The Girl from Dunslaney

Michael D Hopkins

Published in 2023
by © Michael D Hopkins

Paperback Edition
ISBN: 978-1-913898-72-4

Cover and Book interior Design by Russell Holden
www.pixeltweakspublications.com

Pixel Tweaks Publications
SELF PUBLISHING MADE SIMPLE

For Sheila

Chapter One

'Looks like a good summer in store, brother,' remarked James Burton to Sam as they made their way back to the homestead. They'd been checking their snares for rabbits, in the small thicket of trees and bushes bordering the top field. On this occasion their poaching skills had proved fruitless.

'What makes you say that Jim?' enquired Sam.

'The rooks look to be building high, they reckon it's a sign of a good summer,' answered James.

'Seems to me they build high every year,' retorted Sam. 'Can't see how the weather makes any difference.'

The brothers, for whom friendly banter in this vein was their chief mode of communication, had almost reached home. The bells of St. Margaret's church rang in the distance summoning the faithful to Sunday morning worship in the nearby village of Astley. It promised to be a warm and sunny day. The long winter of 1775-76 seemed to be over at last, but pockets of stubborn snow - remnants of the cruel blizzards of March - were still evident in the hedgerows and hollows. Eastertide had been depressingly chilly, but now just three weeks later, nature's yearly miraculous transformation was, at last, well under way. The trees were beginning to assume their green mantle. The fresh smells of spring pervaded the air and the chirruping of the birds, busy with their nest building, seemed to add a special joy to the morning.

Sam, although the younger by eighteen months, was much more outgoing and adventurous than his brother, and just before they arrived home, took James by the arm and said 'How about skipping church for once and having a bit of a lark?'

The ever-cautious James, fearful of the wrath of their God-fearing father and the admonishments of their mother, answered dubiously, 'Why would we do that and risk father's belt? You know he hates us to miss church.'

'Well, we worked hard all week with the spud planting, surely we can have a day off,' offered Sam.

'What for anyway?' asked James.

'I was just thinking about what that old tinker man said when he passed through t'other day, about the boats in the sky.'

'I think he made that up,' scoffed James. 'You know what an old blaggard he is.'

'I still say it'd be worth taking a chance on father's temper' countered Sam. He punched his brother playfully on his arm. 'Come on, Jim, let's do it. I heard it somewhere else about the boats as well.'

* * *

The mighty bridge at Barton, some five miles from the settlement of small farms where the boys lived, had been the talk of the whole community for some time now, although few had actually seen it for themselves. For the most part the local population of staid honest country folk were too engrossed in the daily toil of growing food to feed their families and had neither time nor inclination to venture far afield. Their small farms were situated within the vast estate of the Duke of Bridgewater which lay around the town of Salford.

Seth and Amy Burton were the tenants of one such farm and were into their seventh year of having their own acreage, split into four fields which they farmed diligently. They grew mainly potatoes, oats and barley in rotation to feed their five children. One of the fields was planted with turnips to improve the soil. A few chickens rooted about the farmstead to provide eggs and occasional meat to supplement their plain, monotonous diet. All in all, the never-ending toil involved enabled them to exist adequately, but despite their best efforts they were at the mercy of the elements. A poor summer inevitably led to a hard hungry winter.

Although the younger of the brothers, Sam was already taller and more muscular than James. His mane of thick black hair framed a long, almost oval face. His eyes were also very dark giving him a somewhat brooding countenance, which belied his quick wit and humorous manner. James, in contrast, was of a slimmer wiry build. His hair was the colour of caramel like his mother's. He had recently started to grow a wispy beard, which despite the constant cajoling of his family he steadfastly refused to part with. His constant stroking and scratching of it drove Sam to distraction at times. Since early childhood, Sam had been the undisputed dominant force in their relationship. He could usually bring James round to his will if he tried, and today was no exception.

As the rest of the family prepared for the weekly procession to the small parish church of St. Margaret's, the two lads managed to steal away, their pockets filled with oatmeal cakes, and an apple each from last autumn's dwindling store.

* * *

The five-mile trek was an adventure in itself. In their mundane existence they'd never ventured so far from their home before. They stepped along in lively fashion along old established dirt tracks and fields until they breasted a steep hill and down in the valley below them, they witnessed a breath-taking sight. As far as the eye could see, and in both directions, the canal stretched out before them, the silvery water glistening in the bright sunlight. Even on this day of rest, they watched as three horses plodded along the towpath, attached by a long rope to large barges on the canal, at intervals of a few hundred yards. They made their way down towards the waterside and closer inspection revealed that these barges were all heavily laden with tons of black, shiny coal. The horses seemed to be plodding along almost effortlessly. At the head of each of them was a man controlling their progress.

* * *

As a young buck about London town, Francis Egerton, the Duke of Bridgewater, had courted a beautiful aristocratic lady, but a serious difference of opinion led to the cancellation of the match and he had retired to his country

4

seat, never to return to the delights of high society. Instead, he involved himself wholly in the efficient management of his lands. The main focus of his ambition, however, had been the building of the canal named after him. He owned several coal mines in the Worsley area, which were subject to severe flooding. Navigable underground canals had been constructed in the mines to control the floodwater, and to transport the coal to the surface.

However, the only way to transport the ever-increasing output of coal was by teams of pack horses along rough tracks to the rapidly developing towns of Manchester, Salford, and the port of Liverpool.

In his youth, like so many of the rich young English gentry, the Duke had undertaken "The Grand Tour" of Europe and had been much impressed by the Canal du Midi in the South of France.

He decided to build his own canal to connect Worsley with Manchester to greatly improve the delivery of the product. He'd enlisted the services of one, James Brindley - a canal designer with an already impressive reputation. Between them and the Duke's agent John Gilbert, they had charted the route of the new waterway.

The financing of the project had almost driven the Duke to bankruptcy, but by the time Sam and James set out on their clandestine excursion, the corner had been turned and large profits were being achieved.

The canal had been in constant use for a decade or more. All day long large barges laden with coal plied back and forth. The price of coal fell dramatically, and consumption rose in proportion.

The pre-occupation of the canal and his mines meant that the Duke had delegated the administration of his farming interests to his agents, but he'd never lost his sense of obligation to his scores of tenant farmers. A real rarity among the landowning hierarchy!

* * *

The two lads walked along the towpath for another mile or so until they were confronted by a man blocking their way and indicating that they should divert themselves down a steep embankment to the bank of a fast-flowing river. There, they joined a large crowd of people like themselves, all gathered to see the spectacle of horses and barges apparently walking across the sky.

Mr. Brindley's famous Barton aqueduct, a mighty three-arched construction of bricks and stone built to carry the canal over the River Irwell, had become a talking point throughout the whole country. Large crowds came from far and wide to see this masterpiece of engineering with their own eyes.

James and Sam were totally astonished at the spectacle and stayed for more than two hours, squatting on the bank and eating their food. Boat after boat crossed the wonderful bridge and the lads listened intently to the discussions of total strangers holding forth on what it all meant for the future.

They became aware that the afternoon was passing quickly and so reluctantly they dragged themselves away and began the long walk home, still buzzing with excitement at what they'd seen.

'Who would have thought that such a thing was possible,' said James.

'Hard to believe rightly,' replied his brother, 'but we've seen it with our own eyes, though I don't doubt father will say we've made it up to spare us from his belt.'

It was early evening by the time they arrived back at the farmstead and the lads were anticipating their reception with dread.

In Georgian times, corporal punishment was very much the order of the day even for young adults. A beating would be inflicted if father thought the offence was serious enough to merit it.

They soon found to their cost that their father was in no mood to show leniency.

'So, think you can just skip away just when the mood takes you, do you?' he thundered. 'You need to be taught that it is not so.'

'Please, father,' pleaded Sam. 'It was all my idea, there's no need to chastise James too.'

'Can't we tell you where we've been,' implored James.

'I don't care where you've been,' retorted their irate father. 'You've disappointed me and shown much disrespect to the Lord above. Get outside the pair of you.'

Mother Amy gathered the younger children to her to spare the dignity of the miscreants.

Sam bent over the saw bench first, still hoping that father would show mercy to his brother - alas to no avail.

Seth warmed their posteriors with three lusty blows apiece administered with his thick leather belt, and satisfied that just punishment had been served, he strode back into the cottage.

Although smarting with pain, the brothers' excitement at what they'd witnessed on their excursion was in no way diminished. They regaled their mother and three younger siblings, Angela, John and baby Peter, with the tale of their adventure.

'You should have seen it, Ma,' said James excitedly, 'big heavy boats with piles of coals, and the horses pulling them along with ease.'

'Even so,' replied his mother, 'you had no right to go without father's permission and so you've paid the price, and hopefully learned from it.'

Their humble dwelling was quite spacious by the standards of the day, with a large communal room that was both kitchen and parlour. A stone hearth that was the one source of heat and where all the meals were cooked. The only furniture was a large wooden table and six stools. One of the two further rooms were shared by James, Sam and 12-year-old John. Their parents and 10-year-old Angela slept in the other one along with three-year-old Peter. Their bedding consisted of palliasses stuffed with straw and covered in rough linen.

A lean-to outhouse contained a washtub and wood burning stove, and across the yard was a primitive earth closet over a cesspit.

The next morning the whole family breakfasted on platters of oatmeal porridge as usual, and the talk was once more of the spectacle that the lads had seen.

Seth, although a strict disciplinarian, was also a loving father to his brood, and yesterday's misdemeanours and resulting punishment were swiftly consigned to history.

'Tell me more of this adventure that was worth chastisement,' he said to the brothers.

Sam and James both began to gush forth excitedly.

'Whoa!' said Seth. 'I can't make head or tail of it if you don't slow down. Sam, tell me what you know, and Jimmy hold your tongue.'

Sam did as he was bid, recounting their whole experience from the sight of the endless convoy of barges, the magnificent bridge itself and the crowds who'd come from far and wide to see this modern wonder.

'I've heard talk of these stinking ditches,' remarked Seth, ''tis said they'll soon cover the whole land.'

'Reckon they'll be a good thing too,' offered James.

'They'll bring naught but trouble,' said Seth, 'the gangs of diggers are just drunken thieving Irish rogues who bring fear and destruction to everywhere they go.'

Nothing, however, could dampen the enthusiasm and excitement of the two oldest boys. They went about their daily tasks of hoeing and weeding the bigger field, which had been planted with oats that were already springing up. It was tedious, boring but necessary work to keep the relentless weeds from choking the fresh green shoots. Oatmeal was a huge part of their diet and a decent crop meant the family would not face starvation in the winter, and any surplus could be sold to the estate in part payment of rent.

In the evening the boys walked along the hedgerows and little spinneys setting more snares. It was a skill that had been passed down by Cedric Adnitt, their mother's brother. While strictly speaking poaching was frowned upon by the custodians of the estate, in fact they turned a blind eye to the trapping of rabbits, which were a constant pest. For the local peasantry the rabbits and occasional hare provided a welcome addition to their paltry diet.

The capricious April weather had caused the sky to darken, and a heavy rainfall threatened to soak the lads to the skin. Their meanderings had taken them close to the small church of St. Margaret's in the village of Astley, which served several of the little clusters of dwellings. As they waited in the porch for the storm to pass, they spotted a handbill pinned to the door.

Sam had been taught to read and write by the local cleric, Parson Barlow - a skill he put to use now. He scrutinised the paper closely.

'Well, what does it say?' enquired James, whose reading skills were far behind that of his younger brother.

'It says the Trent and Mersey Canal Company are looking for men to come and dig their new canal with good rates of pay up to two shillings a day,' said Sam, reading haltingly from the hand bill. 'Apply at the Company Office at Preston Brook.'

'Two bob a day!' said James incredulously. 'Have you read that right?'

Sam studied the bill again just to make sure. 'Yeah, that's what it says. What do you think of that?'

'I know what *you're* thinking Sam Burton,' scoffed James, 'and you know as well as I do what father would have to say about it!'

'I don't care what father says,' retorted Sam. 'I reckon I'm going to try it for a while. Plantings all done so he'll manage without me 'til harvest time and he'll surely not refuse the money I'll bring back.'

They arrived home with a pair of rabbits for the pot which was always a guarantee of putting father in an amiable mood, so Sam plunged in and shared his news with his parents. Surprisingly, his father's reaction was not the negative one that James had predicted.

'Sounds too good to be true, lad,' he said, 'but if you think you're fit for it, you might have a go at it. Hopefully you'll bring a nice lot of money back with you. That would be very welcome.'

Their quarterly rent was always a struggle to find. As well as the aforementioned sacks of produce, labouring for the estate at sowing and harvest time was also an acceptable part of the contract.

For some time, Seth had thought about keeping a pig to provide some meat for the family, and some actual coinage would perhaps enable him to do that very thing.

'We'll manage here awhile without you,' said Seth to his second son, 'young John is starting to be useful around the place, so go lad, with my blessing and God go with you.'

So, the next morning, to the tearful farewells of his mother and younger siblings and a hug from his father, young Sam set out on the journey that was to change his life forever.

James joined him for the first mile or so and when they parted it was with a warm embrace, clinging to each other as if they might never meet again.

'Good fortune, brother,' said James, trying to hide the emotion in his voice, and with a final slap on the back Sam was on his way.

* * *

His route took him past where he'd walked with James on the previous Sunday and when he got to the aqueduct, there was no-one this time to hinder his progress across the mighty bridge. As he traversed it, he looked down at the swirling current of the Irwell, swollen by the recent rains. Sam considered the marvels of this tremendous feat of engineering. He was full of admiration for the ingenuity and skill of the man who'd designed it, and the hard and perilous work that had gone into its construction.

He caught up with a horse-drawn barge and asked the man leading the horse if he was heading the right way for Preston Brook.

'Ay lad,' the man replied, 'but it's maybe a dozen miles or more. We're not going all the way today, but we can take you a good bit down t' cut. You'll get a bit grubby from all that coal, mind!'

He slowed the horse down and manoeuvred the barge closer to the bank for Sam to scramble aboard. There was another man standing on top of the coal heap with a long pole, which he used to push the barge back into the middle of the canal.

Sam sat on the back of the pile and thanked God for this lucky break. When he set out, he had no idea of just how far he'd have to travel, and this saving of his weary feet was very welcome.

The pole wielder's job seemed quite demanding - he had to keep the boat firmly in the middle of the course by pushing against the bank if it started to veer off course and there was little time for relaxation.

However, bit by bit Sam managed to ascertain that the load was destined for Runcorn and then by pack horse along the Mersey to Liverpool docks for export. A system of locks to join canal and river was planned but not yet underway.

All afternoon the horse plodded along the towpath and Sam plied Jack the pole man with questions about the working of the system. He found out that the coal was loaded at a wharf adjacent to the Worsley mine and carried either the few miles to Manchester or the twenty-six miles to Runcorn. The longer trip lasted two days with an overnight stop, and the boatmen took it in turns to walk the horse or steer with the pole. They were paid five shillings each for the return trip and they worked pretty much non-stop.

As the sun began to dip Sam could see a cluster of buildings looming into sight.

'This is as far as we go today,' said Jack. ''Tis another fairly long stretch to Preston Brook. You'll not make it before nightfall, so I reckon you'd better stop here with us for the night.'

'I don't have money to pay for lodging,' said Sam anxiously.

'Don't worry about that lad. You can get a bit of grub in yon shed.' Jack pointed to a single storey building separated from the waterside by a cobbled yard, which also contained stabling for the horses.

'You can make a bed in the stable if you can stand the smell of horse shit,' chuckled Ben, the man who'd led the horse all afternoon. 'You can earn your keep by feeding old Noggin and washing him down.'

Sam agreed readily, happy to return the men's hospitality.

The horse had been tethered in a stall in the large stable block. Although he'd had no experience of working with horses, he filled the manger with hay and as the horse fed, he wiped its sweaty flanks with water from the rainwater butt outside.

Satisfied that he'd served the horse well, Sam made his way over to the roomy shed where a dozen or more men were chatting and eating their supper.

A burly woman in a pinafore was ladling out platefuls of a mutton, potato and onion stew, the smell of which filled the young lad's nostrils and reminded him of his ravenous hunger.

'Sit yourself down, my boy,' she said. 'I dare say you could manage a portion of my concoction. It's not as bad as these rapscallions try to make out!'

Sam accepted the heaped plateful gratefully and attacked it with relish. He washed it down with a tankard of strong ale.

Afterwards he sat, in a warm fug of tobacco smoke listening to the tales of the men who spent their lives trudging up and down the length of the Bridgewater canal.

There was much discussion and conjecture on the topic of how canals were being planned to criss-cross the whole country.

As darkness fell, Sam made his way over to the stable and made a bed of hay for himself. Despite the handy lift on the coal barge, his long, exciting day had left him weary, and he was soon fast asleep to the soothing sounds of whinnies and snickering of his roommates!

Thus ended the first day of Sam Burton's new life.

Chapter Two

At about the same time in the spring of 1776, in the town of Enniscorthy in the southeast of Ireland, a young girl was tending her fast-fading mother in the hovel that was their home.

Poor Brigid O'Farrell lay on a bed of straw over which a sheet of coarse linen was spread. Young Mary sat on the low three-legged stool which was the only other piece of furniture. She held a tin mug of water from which she wet Brigid's cracked lips - there was no strength left in the dying woman to take even a sip. The mound of stones with a thin straw roof was the only home that Mary had ever known. There was no door, and the chill evening breeze stirred the meagre smouldering peat fire in the stone hearth, causing the lowly dwelling to fill with smoke once more.

She staggered to the doorway, sobbing pitifully over the latest tragedy to befall her family. She took the fresh bracing air thankfully into her lungs, whilst her mother continued to fight for every breath in the choking gloom.

For all the wretched poverty of her upbringing, Mary O'Farrell was a strikingly pretty girl of seventeen summers, with almost waist-length brown hair and startlingly clear green eyes.

Her father and younger brother had succumbed the previous winter, both stricken by the bronchial chill brought on by the lack of either enough food or warmth to combat the bitter December weather. Most families in that impoverished town were in a similar desperate state. After a few moments of the welcome relief of the cool clear air, Mary returned to the dingy room to hold Brigid's hand and whisper her love. She tried to ignore the dreadful message of her stricken mother's wheezing but could sense that the end was very near.

She felt the feeble pressure of her mother's fingers and leaned in close to her as she tried to speak.

'Ah, Mary my darlin' girl,' she gasped. 'I'm done for. St. Peter is calling me home.'

'Oh, mother,' sobbed Mary, 'don't leave me all alone in the world. What will become of me?'

Mary's prayers for a miracle were in vain, and in the early evening as the soft April light was beginning to fade, Brigid drew her last breath and departed from the misery of her existence.

Half-blinded with grief, Mary staggered outside, to where some of the other poor peasants were gathered. Wailing pitifully, she fell into the arms of her mother's best friend Teresa Turley.

That poor woman, although almost destitute herself, held the heartbroken girl to her bosom. She bade her son Brendan to summon the priest, Father Philip, from the town.

The only place of worship for Catholics in the area was a tiny chapel that had been erected just a few years previously. Only in recent times had the strict anti- Catholic regime been relaxed a little and they were at least able to celebrate Mass.

At length Father Philip arrived at the scene of the latest tragedy to befall his parishioners. He arranged for Brigid's body to be placed in a simple plain coffin and removed to the chapel. There was no money for a proper burial and so the following day like so many of her ilk, Brigid's remains were interred in a pauper's grave.

Father Philip was a tall man whose solemn countenance belied a saintly disposition. He always strove to do his best by his impoverished flock and was much loved and admired by them.

His living, bestowed with some reluctance upon him by the wealthy landowners, the Regan family, enabled him to survive adequately. He had been able to alleviate some of the suffering with the setting up of a soup kitchen for the desperate.

The town of Enniscorthy and all of the surrounding county of Wexford had, like so many parts of Ireland, suffered woefully at the hands of Oliver Cromwell's Parliamentarians over a century before.

In the aftermath of his conquest, a savage subjugation of the mostly Catholic population had occurred. All Catholic churches had been burnt to the ground as punishment for their support of the Royalists in the Civil Wars. In an effort to stamp out Catholicism completely, the celebration of the Mass had been banned. Father Philip was the latest in a long line of priests who had risked their lives to celebrate the Mass in secret hidden places. They were summarily executed if caught – usually burnt at the stake. A scorched earth policy had been ruthlessly applied and all property seized and handed over to Cromwell's English and Anglo-Irish supporters.

Slowly in recent years conditions had started to improve. Some of the better buildings in the town had been restored, and it was beginning to show some semblance of respectability. Goodwill and not a little guilt among some of the more tolerant of the landowners had raised sufficient funds to enable this new small chapel to be built from the ruins of the old one, albeit a much humbler edifice than its predecessor. Catholics were still mostly barred from owning property and most scraped along on a diet consisting mainly of potatoes – just about the only crop that would grow on the poor soil.

Each year the fertility of the land was a little more depleted. The previous harvest had been particularly scant and many of the poor simply starved to death, including all of young Mary's family.

After Brigid's internment he took pity on the grief-stricken girl. He gave her a hot meal of barley soup with scraps of ham and a bed in his small rectory which stood adjacent to the chapel.

The following morning, he took Mary into the town to meet Francis Delaney, to see if he could get her a position up at the castle.

In the market square of the town of Enniscorthy there was an imposing terrace of three-storey houses that had somehow escaped the attentions of Cromwell's marauding troops. Now after some restoration, they served as a rudimentary assemblage of lawyers' offices, counting houses and accommodation for the better off.

One of these was the office of the Dunslaney estate's agent, Francis Delaney, and it was to him that Father Philip brought Mary to appeal for help.

Delaney, a middle-aged portly man, was descended from a family of former Catholics who had converted to Protestantism after Cromwell's savagery.

It had proved to be a prudent move, and for several generations the Delaneys had served the Regans, a Protestant Anglo-Irish family who in the Cromwell era, had been granted a huge swathe of land in the proximity of Enniscorthy town.

The Regans had flourished in the hundred years and more since. The fertile land was stocked with herds of beef and dairy cattle. The Regan dynasty had grown rich on the production of salt beef, pork, cheeses and grain, mostly exported across the Irish sea. The labour required had been provided by the local peasantry for little or no reward apart from a hovel to live in and a patch of land to grow potatoes.

A few of the bolder among the peasantry managed to pilfer some of the produce to supplement their meagre diet, but it was an enterprise full of risk. Eviction or worse was the fate of any caught committing such a heinous crime.

Their wealth had enabled the Regans to restore a large country house that had stood since the Norman Conquest, with the grand title Dunslaney Castle.

A small army of domestic staff ranging from lowly stable lads and gardeners to scullery maids, chamber maids, a housekeeper and butler, serviced every whim of their masters, providing a little relief from the grinding poverty for the fortunate few.

The current incumbent was Fintan Regan, a tall, handsome man of swarthy countenance. Now in his mid-thirties, he'd inherited the property after his father Gerard had drunk himself into an early grave.

Fintan's whole life had been one of carefree abandon - the rich country squire whose days were spent hunting and shooting. He possessed, too, a flair for fencing with some of the other dashing young bucks of the county set.

There were several other affluent households in the county. Fintan Regan was considered to be the prize catch by all the matriarchs of these families, but so far, he had resisted their attempts at trying to furnish him with a wife.

Despite the advantages of great wealth, he had spent a somewhat solitary childhood. There were no siblings and he'd been virtually ignored by his father, who held him responsible for the death of Fintan's mother, Roisin.

A long painful confinement had led to a fever from which she'd never recovered. Gerard Regan was consumed with grief. He'd loved his slender wife with an ardent passion and was given to bouts of uncontrolled fury at his hapless infant child. So concerned were the senior domestic staff at the illogical manifestation of their master's grief, that they took steps to ensure the baby was kept well away from his father's malevolence.

A series of tutors, riding instructors, fencing masters and the like had provided the young man with an excellent education and he strode through life without a care in the world. The bewilderment and hurt caused by his father's indifference to him slowly diminished as he matured, but their estrangement grew ever wider.

A half-hearted attempt at reconciliation by Gerard when he had become aware that his remaining days were few, had been greeted with barely concealed contempt and suspicion by his son.

On the very afternoon that his father had breathed his last, Fintan was out with some friends shooting wildfowl on the river and had to be persuaded to make haste and return to the castle for the sake of propriety.

He displayed an air of casual impassivity to the daughters of the Co. Wexford mothers, to the despair of the latter. No matter how beguiling and winsome the never-ending line of potential brides, he'd so far managed to evade ensnarement.

He much preferred the local peasant girls of whom he had his pick, thanks to his procurer Delaney.

* * *

When he first caught sight of the pretty ragamuffin that the priest had brought to him, Delaney's first lascivious thought was that she would be of great interest to Fintan Regan. With her long flowing locks and green eyes, he could see that it would be yet another feather in his cap, to present such an appetising dish before the master. He had no designs on the girl for himself - his sexual preferences lay in a completely opposite direction.

Duly, he thanked the priest and told him that he would take Mary up to the castle where there was a vacancy for a maid.

Mary, bewildered and bereft as she was, could hardly take in what had happened to change her life so swiftly.

She took a tearful farewell of Father Philip and followed Delaney into the house, which was both office and spacious living accommodation.

He instructed his housekeeper, Mrs Hartnett, to feed the girl and give her a hot bath. He had prudently laid in a store of women's attire for the very purpose of making them more attractive to Mr. Regan and could see that Mary's inherent prettiness would be much enhanced with some better apparel.

The warm water of the first bath she'd ever had left Mary glowing with a feeling of optimism for whatever lay ahead. The kindly Mrs Hartnett found a bodice, skirt and shawl for her and soon she was led back into Delaney's office.

He caught his breath in admiration at the young vision of loveliness standing before him. Despite his avowed lack of desire for womankind in matters of the heart, even he could recognise natural beauty when he saw it. She'd fit the bill very well.

'Now, girl,' he said, adopting a firm but gentle tone, 'I know how much you're grieving for your lost family, but you must learn to put it all behind you. There's a whole new life waiting for you up at the castle.'

'Thank you, sir,' replied Mary, full of doubt, 'but I have no idea if I would be able for the position, and how am I to get there?'

'Don't worry about that, you'll soon learn what's required of you,' Delaney replied. 'Normally, I'd say you'd have to walk, 'tis only four miles. However, I've business there this afternoon, so I'll take you in my gig.'

Mary, for whom every hour seemed to be bringing more new experiences, sat stiffly beside him in his handsome gig for the journey to Dunslaney and her new life.

Delaney set his pony to, what was to Mary, a perilously fast trot along a road that was little more than a rutted grass track. She clung on grimly to the door of the little gig and braced her feet firmly against the floor.

Delaney laughed at her obvious alarm and said, 'Don't worry, my dear, you're perfectly safe. My wee Gracie knows every pothole and bump between here and the castle.'

Eventually, much to her relief, the turrets and towers of Dunslaney castle could be seen through the tall elm and oak trees, and as they drew near Mary gaped in awe at the sheer size of it. She'd never been more than a couple of miles from her humble dwelling before and the magnificent limestone walls seemed to glow in the clear spring sunlight.

Delaney drove up the avenue to the massive double oak doors. He handed her down from the gig. She hesitantly approached the entrance, but he pulled her away and led her around to the left of the building to a much smaller door.

'This is the way in and out for you, girl,' he chuckled, 'at least until you become a fine lady.'

He led her along a stone flagged passage to a large kitchen, which seemed to Mary a hive of industry. Half a dozen people were busy at various tasks around a large wooden table. A skinny tall woman of middle years eyed her up and down and sniffed dramatically, as if she could smell something obnoxious about the girl.

'Mrs Molloy,' said Delaney, 'I'm sure you can find work for an extra pair of hands, so I'll leave this lass to you.'

Turning to the young girl, he said 'Goodbye, Mary. Do as you're bid, and you'll get along just fine. You'll have to work hard, but you'll eat well and have a roof over your head. Good luck to you.'

With that he was gone, leaving Mary to the ordeal of inspection from her new colleagues.

'Over here, girl,' ordered Mrs Molloy, somewhat haughtily. 'Let's have a look at you in the light. Sure, there's not a pick on you, I can see you need fattening up a bit.'

'Sit down there,' she pointed to a stool by the table.

'Here's a drop of mutton stew, for you. Eat that, and I'll show you your duties.'

Mary, who'd rarely eaten meat in her whole life, ate the tasty dish of stew, trying hard not to wolf it down too quickly.

'Looks like you enjoyed that, Miss,' said a young lad who appeared to be a little younger than herself. 'I'm Henry. They call me a junior footman, but it's just a grand name for general dogsbody. I'm at everybody's beck and call.'

'Be quiet, Henry,' scolded the woman. 'Ye've a roof over your head, just be thankful for it.'

When Mary had finished eating Mrs Molloy said, 'Right, let's see what you're worth, my girl. Come with me.'

She led the girl back up the long passage and into the main building. They went through a door off the vast, high-ceilinged entrance hall into a large room furnished with various chairs and tables. A chaise longue stood in front of a huge fireplace. Mary gazed around in awe – she'd had never seen anything as fabulously luxurious in all her young life.

'Now as you can see,' said Mrs Molloy, 'this is called the drawing room where the master entertains his friends, and it's in need of a good clean up. You can start by clearing the fireplace and laying the coals.'

'I've never done anything like this before,' stuttered Mary.

'Ach there's nothing to it. Just clean everything that looks in need of it,' replied Mrs Molloy. 'Come back with me and I'll get you the things you'll need.'

Mary returned armed with a broom, pan and dusters, and set about the task she'd been given. She realised that this was a test and so she fell to it with gusto.

She began by clearing the ashes from the grate and laying kindling of paper and sticks. Then she began to dust some of the many ornaments, portraits of stern-faced Regan ancestry and various other wall hangings, humming softly to herself as she did so.

'Are you enjoying yourself, macushla?' said a booming voice behind her.

She turned with a start and saw a tall gentleman who had entered the room, immaculately dressed in a dark blue tailcoat and cream-coloured breeches.

She curtseyed and turned bright scarlet as he fixed her with an appraising stare.

'Have ye no tongue in your head, lass?' he said playfully.

Mary was by now completely dumb struck, not a word could she utter.

'Come now, girl, at least tell me your name.'

'Tis Mary, sir,' she managed to stutter at last.

'Ah sweet Mary, a lovely name for a wholesome young girl. Now tell me what a pretty maid like you is doing in my house. I've never seen you before?'

'Please sir, Mr Delaney brought me here and said I would find work,' answered Mary, shyly.

Regan gave her a warm smile and said, 'So be it. I will not hold you back. Mr Delaney is usually very astute, so I'm sure you'll do well. Be sure not to break anything, won't you.'

With that he turned and left the flustered young girl to complete her work.

Thus was Mary introduced to Fintan Regan - the man who was to have such a profound effect on her future.

Chapter Three

Over the course of the following days, under the guidance of Elidh Molloy, Mary began to settle into her new life. There was no time to dwell on her grief and sense of loss. She had to work all day from early morning until late in the evening, with little respite. At least she was eating properly for the first time in her life. The regular and ample diet began to add weight and strength to her already comely figure.

Despite her gruff and sardonic nature, Mrs Molloy was a kindly soul, who had taken to Mary - just one more in a line of waifs and strays who'd found their way to the castle.

She could see that Mary had the makings of a hard-working diligent lass, who was quick to learn and eager to please.

Sadly, she guessed at the fate that lay in store for her - it was a well-established routine. Delaney supplied only the prettiest of the local peasant girls for his master's pleasure, and there was always a new one to take the place of the incumbent, when Regan tired of her.

In a roundabout way, Elidh tried to warn Mary of the ordeal that lay ahead of her, but her own position was precarious enough. There was little she could do to forestall the probability of Mary's seduction and violation at the master's hands.

* * *

Regan, having been brought up in a cocoon of luxurious but solitary idleness, knew or cared little for the source of his wealth. The administration of his businesses he left in the hands of Delaney and various accountants and lawyers.

He knew that one day he would have to marry and produce an heir but put that thought to the back of his mind. He could count on the ever-reliable Delaney to feed his voracious sexual appetite.

Some of his conquests had not been difficult - girls that knew the lie of the land and submitted resignedly. Others had offered him stout resistance. It was the latter that gave him most pleasure, breaking them to his will as he would a foal or young hound.

His current bed wench was an earthy ginger head named Dena. She was proving to be quite the best ride he'd had for a while, matching his lustful appetite with considerable relish

However, as was his habit, he began to tire of her both physically and mentally. The new girl Mary had taken his eye immediately and he was already anticipating the pleasure of making her his latest conquest.

He bade Mrs Molloy to send word to Delaney that he needed to see him, so she sent young Joe, a stable hand, to deliver the message.

When Delaney arrived, he approached Regan cautiously, always on his guard in case he'd done something amiss.

'Ah, Francis,' boomed Regan.

Delaney breathed a sigh of relief. It was always a good sign when the master used his Christian name.

'The trollop Dena,' he said. 'She's outstayed her welcome. Give her three guineas and take her to Peg Mulvaney.'

'Very good, sir,' replied Delaney. 'I'll do it straight away.'

Peg Mulvaney ran a bawdy house in the dock area of the town of Wexford, a few miles to the east. It was where Regan's cast-offs were usually sent. What befell them after that was of no concern to either Regan or Delaney.

Dena grudgingly accepted her fate. A worldly girl, she knew her time was up as soon as the new girl had appeared in the servant's quarters, even if the innocent young Mary had no inkling of what Regan had in mind for her.

'So, that's it for me, is it?' she sneered angrily to Delaney. 'His Lordship has had his fill and I'm to be cast off like a worn-out cloak.'

'That's the way of it madam,' answered Delaney. 'Think yourself lucky. Surely you knew it wasn't going to last for ever. You're better off than most. He's found a place for you in the town.'

Delaney took her to Mulvaney's door and gave her a guinea coin. The rest of her "severance pay" went into his own pocket.

'Here we are now. Out you get,' he said brusquely. 'I'm sure Mistress Mulvaney can find a position for you.'

Dena had no idea where she was being escorted to, but one look at the blowsy countenance of Madam Mulvaney and the scent of cheap perfume wafting from the house behind her was enough for the penny to swiftly drop. She shouted foul curses at the rapidly vanishing Delaney, but nevertheless she entered Peg Mulvaney's house, and her new role in life.

* * *

Back at the castle Regan was planning his seduction of the young girl. It was a game he enjoyed almost as much as the act itself.

He gave instructions to Mrs. Molloy that Mary was to become his chamber maid and was to attend to his personal needs.

Elidh had seen it all before, of course, and although she feared for Mary and how such an innocent young creature would cope, there was precious little she could do. It was just the way of the world - the rich always held the winning cards.

She could only hope that the girl wouldn't catch for a child - there had been enough "accidents" of that sort in the past as she knew only too well. She tried to envisage a way of saving her from the bawdy house after Regan tired of her, as he inevitably would.

When she told Mary that Regan had praised her work and that she was to become his personal maid, she was surprised by the girl's calm reaction. It was as if she'd guessed what would be expected of her and was ready to accept her fate stoically.

For the first few days nothing untoward happened to her. Regan hardly acknowledged her presence as she went about her duties. Cleaning and polishing industriously, preparing the majestic four poster bed, and emptying the chamber pot, just grateful for the new chance she'd been given.

Things changed dramatically on the fourth day in her new role. Regan returned from the hunt covered in mud. Several servants brought a hip bath and pitchers of hot water to the bedchamber. When the bath was filled, Regan dismissed them all except Mary.

'Help me off with these boots and britches, girl,' he commanded brusquely.

She did as he ordered and then he stripped off the rest of his underclothes to stand naked before her. She turned bright crimson at the sight of his naked body and despite herself, her eyes were drawn to his manhood - the first time she'd ever seen such a thing.

'Stop your gawking girl and give me your arm,' he ordered.

Averting her eyes, Mary helped him to clamber into the bath. She turned to leave hoping to escape, but he bade her to stay.

'Nothing to fear my dear,' he said in a softer tone. 'I just want you to get this accursed mud off my back.'

She did so, demurely sponging his back with the soapy water, praying that her discomfiting ordeal would soon be over. Regan, however, had other plans. Deftly he seized her arm and plunged it into the bath, guiding her hand to his now erect penis. She tried to snatch it away, but his grip was too strong, and he made her hold it for several seconds as it swelled even more in her soft hand.

Eventually she managed to wriggle free and ran sobbing from the chamber.

Next door, in Regan's dressing room, Mary sat on a stool in a state of panic. She realised that if she fled altogether, it would mean she would be dismissed and put out to face destitution on the roads.

In her innocence, she'd never given a thought to what went on between grown men and women. Her introduction to the world of sexual relations had been forthright and startling, causing her to tremble in shock and fear. From her lowly status in life, she had never dreamt that she would be of any interest to a man like the master, and now she sat in dread of what was to happen next.

The bedroom door opened, and Regan slipped casually into the room and stood over her. He was dressed in just a silken gown. Swiftly he pulled her to her feet and wrapped his strong arms around her slender body.

'Dear, sweet girl,' he murmured in her ear. 'I am sorry if my behaviour shocked you. It was an impulse brought on by my proximity to quite the loveliest creature I've ever seen. You have no idea of the effect you're having on me.'

The traumatised maiden had no idea of how to respond. Her body became stiff with tension. He began to stroke her long brown hair and tilted her face to his and placed his mouth on hers. Unsure how to respond, she parted her lips slightly and experienced her first ever adult kiss. Despite her confusion, she felt a tingle of excitement flowing through her veins. His lips seemed almost glued to hers and she could feel the tip of his tongue trying to explore inside her mouth.

She felt powerless to resist his embrace and she realised he was pulling her back towards the bed chamber. He pushed her down onto the four poster and shrugged off his robe. She got a glimpse of his fully erect member and closed her eyes tightly. He lifted her skirt to reveal her naked thighs. The poorer class women of the time never knew the luxury of underwear so there was no further hindrance to his endeavours.

It had all happened so quickly, and she lay semi-paralysed in fear. Realising, at last, what he was going to do she began to struggle but Regan's lustful desire had given him extra strength and Mary gasped in shock and pain as her hymen was ruptured and he forced himself inside her. He began to thrust vigorously causing her to squeal in distress. Her hapless struggling and yelps of pain inflamed him even more, but thankfully his urgent desire drove him quickly to his climax. He withdrew abruptly and she felt the warm spurt of his seed against the inside of her thigh.

He rolled away from her and lay on his back beside her, panting with the exertion of his defilement of his victim.

'My God, Mary that was wonderful,' he panted. 'I'm sorry if it hurt you, but don't worry, the next time won't be as painful, and trust me, you'll begin to enjoy it too.'

Mary turned away from him and sobbed quietly into the pillow. Full of shame and disgust, she knew there was no help or comfort to be had from any outside source and as long as she remained here, she would be at his mercy.

Presently she heard his soft snoring and rose from the bed as quietly as she could, lest he awoke and took her again.

Gathering her dishevelled garments around her she staggered out into the dressing room and wiped the mess of her blood and his semen from her thighs as best she could using only her hand.

She made her way slowly down the back staircase and into the kitchen. One look at the wretched girl's stricken face was enough to show Mrs Molloy what had happened.

Elidh Molloy had seen it all before, but there was something in the sweet innocence of this poor lass, so pitilessly taken from her, that tugged at Elidh's heartstrings.

Off the kitchen was the washroom where a copper boiler was always kept full of hot water. She scooped a big jugful into a bowl.

'Come in here, lass,' she said. 'Let's get you clean.'

'What for?' sobbed Mary, bitterly. 'Just so he can do it again.'

There was little Elidh could say or do to alter the truth in Mary's realisation of her fate, but she felt she had to try anyway.

'Trust me, you will feel better when you're washed. Come on and I'll brush that lovely hair of yours too.'

Apart from Father Philip's ministrations, it was one of the first acts of genuine kindness that Mary had ever received. In the hardship of her tragic upbringing there had been no time for displays of affection, and despite her misery, she felt herself warming to the older woman.

On her arrival at the castle, her first impression of the housekeeper was that she was a humourless harridan and Mary had been resolved to keep well out of the way of her. As the days passed though, she could see there was another side to Elidh. The way in which she'd tried to comfort her after her ordeal made Mary realise that she had found a true friend.

Back in the kitchen, Elidh said 'Sit you down here acushla, 'til I make you some sweet tea. 'Tis a cruel world and you must learn to bear it. You're not the first and I doubt you'll be the last. He'll tire of you soon enough, just beg him not to spend inside you.'

'I hate him,' cried Mary fiercely. 'I'll not let him get away with it. So help me, I'll find a way to make him pay.'

'Keep those ideas to yourself, girl,' warned Elidh. 'If he hears of anything like that, you'll be out on your ear. Bide your time, you never know what fate has in store.'

Despite the gentle assistance of the older woman, Mary spent a largely sleepless night in the garret she shared with two other servant girls. Ashamed and appalled, recalling every last second of the assault, she lay trembling in fear of being summoned to the master's bedchamber again.

Thankfully, her fears were unfounded - at least for the time being.

The next day, on a bright chilly morning, she attended her master as he took breakfast in his bedchamber. Regan virtually ignored her presence - there was no mention of the previous night's events.

She did her best to control the trembling in her hands as she went about her tasks. He rose from the small table where he had taken his food and rang a bell to summon Elidh.

'Mrs Molloy,' he addressed the housekeeper as she hovered uncertainly in the doorway. 'I have business in the town and will not be back until eventide. Have Joseph bring Prince to the front door in half an hour.'

With that he dismissed both the women and attended to his morning ablutions, without a second glance at the young maid who he had deflowered so callously.

Mary watched from the window, with bitter resentment, as her tormentor mounted the handsome horse and trotted off along the drive.

She carried out her work mechanically, with the realisation that this was no longer the chief reason for her appointment here. She was to be his bed wench - at his beck and call, whenever the fancy took him

The power of the sun's rays had soon taken the chill from the air to leave a beautiful spring morning. When she'd finished her tasks, she said to Mrs Molloy, 'Will it be alright if I take a walk round outside. I feel the need for some fresh air?'

'You can, of course,' replied the older woman. 'Don't be too long mind, there is plenty I can find you to do here.'

In the two weeks since her mother's passing, she'd had little time to dwell on the loss of her whole family. This was the first time she'd been allowed to stroll around the huge estate that surrounded the house. Some of the fields were already clothed in a green blanket of young wheat, barley and oats, whilst in others, cattle and sheep were grazing.

At length she came to a large stable yard and encountered the young lad who'd brought Regan's horse to the main house.

'Hello, Mary,' he said shyly.

He was a slightly built lad of about the same age as herself, with straw coloured hair and a pale freckled face.

'How do you know my name?' she asked. 'I've never met you before.'

'My sister Elidh told me,' he replied.

Mary was perplexed. 'Oh, Mrs Molloy is your sister, then? I never knew. It's just she seems a lot older.'

'She is, surely, but that is the way of it. She is all the family I have.'

'Seems we're alike in that way,' said Mary. 'I have no-one in the world, my family have all been taken to Heaven.'

Joseph seemed a little embarrassed to be talking to this beautiful lass and went on forking hay into a stall.

'Have ye been here long?' asked Mary.

'All my life,' Joe replied, 'I was born here.'

'Is that so. Well, who would have thought it.'

'It's not so strange. My mother died when I was just a wee child. I never knew my father, and Elidh never talks about him.'

Mary considered these snippets of information and said 'It's time I was heading back. It was nice to meet you. It's Joseph your name so?'

'It is, but everybody calls me Joe,' replied the lad.

'I'll come again maybe when I get the chance,' said Mary, 'but I have to get back now, or I won't be allowed out again.'

'Do so, Mary, whenever you can,' said Joe, hesitantly. 'We can be friends if it pleases you.'

'Oh yes indeed,' said Mary. 'I have no friends, so that would be a nice thing for both of us.'

She hurried back to the castle to find that the kitchen was the usual scene of bustling activity. Elidh was sitting at the kitchen table polishing the silver cutlery and two other maids, Rosie and Winnie were peeling onions and potatoes. Young Henry was busy cleaning the master's boots.

'I've just been talking to young Joe,' said Mary. 'He told me that he's your brother.'

'Yes, that's right,' replied Elidh abruptly.

'It just seems a bit strange that he never comes near the kitchen or mingles with anybody.'

'He likes to keep himself to himself. He just lives for the horses, really. He don't mix with other folk too well.'

Mary sensed that the older woman seemed uneasy at being quizzed and so she decided not to press her further.

The young girl was dreading the return of Regan, but surprisingly he never sent for her that evening or indeed for the next two.

She began to hope that he was satisfied with stealing her maidenhood and would not bother her again, but it turned out to be a false assumption.

On the third evening she was sitting in the kitchen with a bowl of broth, when Mrs Molloy told her she was bidden to go to his chamber. With a heavy sense of foreboding, she approached the dressing room. Regan was sitting on a sofa before the fireplace.

She could sense that he had been drinking as usual, from his rumpled appearance and demeanour.

'Ah Mary,' he mumbled incoherently. 'Fairest maid in all the land. Come sit by me girl.'

Resignedly, she did as she was bid. Immediately he pulled her to him and lowered his mouth to hers. She was repulsed by his alcoholic breath, but realised she had no choice but to submit to his clumsy advances with a semblance of willingness. She tried to imagine that she was outside of her of her body, and that these things were happening to someone else.

He began to undo the fastenings of her bodice, and after fumbling ineffectually for a while ordered her to do it herself.

'For God's sake girl,' he said, his voice throaty with lust. 'Take the damn things off.'

Primly, she did as she was bid and tried to cover herself with her hands. Regan forcefully pulled her hands away and fell on her pert upturned breasts ravenously sucking them in turn.

'Lie down on the rug,' he commanded her.

She complied and lay flat on her back on the coarse reed rug in front of the fireplace. He climbed on top of her and once again without further ceremony he lifted her skirt and entered her forcefully. She gasped at the vigour of his onslaught - unlike the first time she felt no pain as such, but the heat from the fire and the coarse fibres of the rug beneath her caused her much discomfort as he pounded away clutching her shoulders fiercely. Mercifully his lustful thrusts quickly drove him to a moaning shuddering climax, but on this occasion, he didn't withdraw at the last moment and spent his copious seed inside her.

'Jesus, sweet lass,' he gasped, as he rolled off her. 'You turn me into a man possessed. You've worn me out again so quickly.'

With that, he closed his eyes and fell asleep immediately on the rug.

Mary lay for a few moments, ashamed and disgusted. Her dismay was compounded by the fact that she knew that this was to be her lot in life. Abused and violated - forever at her master's call when the mood took him, and then to be cast aside when a new maid was procured for him by the ever-obliging Delaney.

She waited until she was sure he was sound asleep and then rose from the fireside, wiped herself and tiptoed from the room. Her only consoling thought was that maybe the monster might be consumed or at least scorched by the fire as he lay snoring loudly.

Dreading his waking lest he demanded a repeat performance, she went through to the outer chamber. She noticed that on the dressing table he'd left some coins and a pocket watch. A germ of an idea was planted in her brain.

Chapter Four

The following morning dawned dismal and damp on the Bridgewater Canal - more akin to November than May.

Sam was invited to continue his ride on the coal barge, and he made a bedraggled figure, sitting astride the tons of coal.

They'd made an early start just as dawn was breaking and after a couple of hours of steady plodding, they had travelled a few more miles and Sam could see another cluster of buildings on the horizon. The crew had changed jobs and so it was Jack who slowed the horse enough for Sam to scramble from the barge on to the towpath.

'That's where you're headed, boy' said Jack, pointing at the buildings about half a mile distant. 'Tis where the new cut starts.'

'They reckon it'll be near a hundred miles long when it's finished. Going right down south to a place called Stoke and beyond,' called Ben from atop the pile of coal.

Sam thanked both men warmly. They both wished him luck and he set off down the path at a brisk pace to meet his destiny, quickly leaving the plodding horse and crew behind.

In no time at all he came to where the two canals were going to merge, although the join had not yet been made.

He picked his way over the strip of land that was all that separated the Bridgewater from the new cut and approached the first of the buildings. The door was ajar, so he knocked and timidly walked in. A grey-haired bespectacled man was poring over some papers on a huge wooden table.

'Yes, young man, what can I do for you?' enquired the man peering over his glasses that had slid down his nose.

'Please sir,' said Sam, nervously. 'I saw a poster that said there was work available here.'

'Aye, lad, there is and plenty of it,' answered the man.

He looked Sam up and down appraisingly and said 'You look fit and strong. Are ye used to hard work?'

'Yes, sir. Brought up to it on the farm,' said Sam proudly.

'Can you read and write?'

'Yes sir.'

He opened a huge ledger that was sitting on the table.

Handing Sam a quill and inkpot, he said 'Write your name, age and where you're from in this book.'

Sam did as he was bid, in his slow and painstaking style.

'Right, Sam,' said the older man. 'We'll give ye a start, but I warn you it's damned hard work. If you don't measure up, you'll be out soon enough. Show me your boots.'

Sam lifted his foot up on to a bench.

'Oh, my dear boy!' said the man, sternly. 'They'll not last you here for more than a week. Come with me.'

He led Sam across a yard containing a variety of well-made brick buildings, one of which was obviously a store, where all manner of tools, implements and other accessories were on display, including a whole rack of stout leather boots.

'Find a pair that fit well lad. Most important to have good stout boots,' said the man.

'I have no money to pay for new boots,' said Sam.

The man smiled and said 'They're four shillings a pair and you can pay a shilling a week for four weeks. If you last that long.'

After a while Sam found a pair that fitted adequately.

'Right,' said the man. 'My name is Peter Davies, and you come to me if there's anything you need.'

He selected a long-handled spade, which he gave to Sam.

'That's all you'll need for now, Sam. Come with me and I'll take you to the diggings.'

Sam fell into step, and they began to walk along a completed stretch of the new canal. It was just a wide dry trench at a depth of about five feet, but it had been carefully laid and the sides squared up. The drizzly rain had turned into a steady downpour, making the pathway soft and slippery in places.

After a few hundred yards they came to where the work in the next section was underway.

To Sam, the scores of men swarming like ants over the terrain as far as the eye could see was a bewildering sight.

'It may look like chaos at first sight,' said Mr. Davies, 'but it all fits together as you'll see presently.'

A tall well-built man of middle years made his way towards them.

'Ah. Mr Davies,' he said. 'Is this a new pair of hands for me, for I'm in sore need?'

'It is, indeed, George, he's called Sam and he looks a good prospect.'

'Sam,' said Davies, 'this is your foreman Mr. Medlock. Do as he bids you, work hard and we'll see how you get on.'

At first Sam felt a little trepidation in the presence of Medlock. He considered himself tall and well-built, but beside this giant of a man he felt quite stunted. Nonetheless, as he was to find out over the next few months, George Medlock was a tough but fair man and was to play a major role in his future.

'Reet lad,' he said in a broad Yorkshire accent, 'let's get thee started.'

Medlock led Sam to where a group of four men were working.

'Right men, this our new man, Sam. Break him in gently, 'til we see if he's any good.'

Turning to Sam he said, 'This is where you start to earn thy wages, lad. Take thy spade and start digging where Matt here tells you.'

Matt Docherty and his brother Tom were two Irishmen from Donegal, and along with their cousin Gerard Mulryan and another local Cheshire man, Jack Willett, formed Medlock's gang.

'Right Sam,' said Matt. 'Just start digging and fill yon barrow. When it's full, push it to yon plank - walk behind us and Jack will take it from you. Wait 'til he's emptied it then bring it back and start again.'

Sam, struggling at first with Matt's impenetrable Donegal brogue, did as he was bid and toiled hard, determined to make a good impression.

'Oy, slow down a bit boy,' warned Matt's brother Tom. 'Medlock sees you going at it like that, he'll have us all at it.'

Over the course of the morning Sam filled the barrow over and over until he thought his back was breaking. His palms began to develop blisters and he was relieved to hear Medlock shouting to his gang. 'Down tools men. Grub's arrived.'

Sam looked up to see three women walking along the path to the dig, bearing a large pot of hot broth and loaves of bread on a handcart. A second cart was laden with pitchers of ale. The men queued up to receive a dish of the vegetable and barley soup and a hunk of bread. They hunkered down wherever they could and ate quickly, relishing the tasty food. Sam, whose morning's hard work had given him a mighty appetite, quickly finished his food and one of the women beckoned for him to come back for more which he accepted gratefully. A big tankard of ale to slake his massive thirst was a welcome addition.

All too soon it was back to the digging. All afternoon they toiled away following a carefully pegged out line, creating a trench that was over five feet deep and eight yards wide. Jack Willet and the other men took stints of an hour or so each at the hazardous task of pushing the barrow up the ramp, where other men loaded the spoil into horse drawn carts to be carried away and used on other sections for embankments and other earthworks.

The ramp was just two long planks lashed together with rope and very soon became treacherously slippery. It was washed down every so often but soon became covered in mud again, sometimes causing the laden barrows to slide off the ramp, tip over and deposit their load on the floor of the dig. They would have to be refilled and placed on the plank ramp again. A frustrating experience which was to happen to Sam on more than one occasion.

The rain had stopped by late morning, but the ground beneath their feet had become a quagmire. The sun had come bursting through the clouds beating down on the toiling men. Sam was just about on his knees with exhaustion when at long last Medlock came up and called for a halt to the day's proceedings.

The men began to trudge the half mile or so back to the compound of buildings. They walked for some of the way back along the trench they had dug, but then had to scrabble up onto the pathway which ran alongside the completed section, because another gang of men were still working at where the new canal would eventually be joined to the Bridgewater.

These men, or so it seemed to Sam, were engaged in some kind of strange ritual, stamping their feet hard into the ground.

Noticing Sam's perplexed look, Medlock laughed. 'They're not dancing lad, they're puddling. It's a pleasure you've got coming your way.'

'It's a mix of clay and loam,' he continued, 'then it's mixed with water to form a seal to stop leakage. The only way to put it down is with thy feet and spade.'

'You think digging's hard, boy?' added Mulryan. 'Wait 'til you try this.'

Sam grimaced at the thought that there could be an even worse job than the one he'd been at all day, but he was determined to stick at it, whatever challenges were thrown his way.

* * *

They reached the compound, to one side of which were a row of canvas tents and makeshift huts made of timber and old sheets of iron, which proved to be the men's living accommodation.

After another meal exactly the same as the one served earlier with more ale, the men sat around a huge campfire smoking pipes and quaffing even more of the strong, hoppy ale to wash away the memory of the day's toil.

Medlock, seeing that Sam seemed uncertain of where his place was in the ensemble addressed his gang.

'Come on lads, make room for t' young 'un. He didn't fare too bad now did he?'

Then to Sam he said, 'Go see the women and get thysen a bucket of briny water to soak thy hands. It'll help with t' blisters.'

As the light of the lengthy May Day gradually faded to dusk, the men drifted one by one into the tents and huts to doss down for the night.

After soaking his hands for a while, Sam was allocated a palliasse in one of the huts along with three other men including Matt Docherty, who fell asleep immediately, snoring loudly.

Sam thought it strange that the other members of the work gang weren't there too but found out the next day that the three women who had served their victuals were the wives of the other three men and had separate sleeping quarters. Despite the strangeness of his new surroundings, the snoring and mutterings of his bedfellows, and the hardness of his bedding, Sam quickly dropped off into deep sleep, worn out by the exertions of his first day's toil as a "navvy".

* * *

Meanwhile over the sea in Co. Wexford, Mary was forlornly enduring the almost nightly assaults of her master. There was little attempt at endearment from him, he just used her body for his lustful gratification. She had no choice but to appease him. It was always an urgent, almost brutal coupling with no variation. Thankfully he never again spent inside her, always withdrawing at the critical moment and she became inured to the indignity of his semen splashed over her stomach or thighs.

Her only relief came when she entreated him for a break when her monthly bloods had arrived.

Regan dismissed her peevishly, as if she'd brought on her menstrual cycle just to displease him. Despite the discomfort of her period pains and having to deal with heavy bleeding, which she staunched with linen rags from the kitchen, she used the welcome break to become more friendly with young Joe the stable lad.

She'd join him whenever she could snatch a few minutes from her household duties. There were quite a number of horses in the yard. Some were big shires for farm work and others smaller ponies for the carriages and gigs. The pride of the stables were the hunters. Three magnificent stallions: Duke a young four-year-old with a black shiny coat; then Baron, an older grey horse.

The pick of the bunch, undoubtedly, was a handsome chestnut six-year-old of 16 hands with a white blaze. His name was Prince, and he was Regan's pride and joy.

Mary loved to watch Joe at his work. He was obviously a very conscientious and experienced worker with a natural love and understanding of his charges.

Joe wasn't the only stable hand - there were two more that were both older than him, but they both seemed a bit dull and backward and it was Joe they looked to for instructions

Mary, despite her impoverished background, was a spirited intelligent lass, and she was puzzled as to why a lad so young seemed to have the run of the stables.

'Do they leave you in charge of all these horses Joe?' she enquired. 'It seems a lot for a young lad to do.'

'Well, there's Dan and Seamus as well,' he answered, 'but they just do what I tell them.'

'My Granda was the head groom and he taught me all I know. He died a while ago, so they just left me to it. It just comes natural like. Grandma died not long after Granda. I moved out of their cottage and just stay in the stable now. My sister brings me my food or sometimes when master's not about, I go to the kitchen.'

'I just love horses better than folk,' he added.

'Don't you like the master, then?' asked Mary.

'I hate the bastard,' he hissed forcibly, 'lording it over everybody as if he's God Almighty.'

'Has he ever beaten you?' said Mary.

'Ay, he raises his crop sometimes, 'specially when he thinks I haven't turned Prince out properly for him.'

Mary stored this information in her memory, for she was trying to find a way out of her awful predicament and realised that Joe, for all his youth would make a powerful ally.

As the month of May dragged inexorably on, and Regan's callous use of her became a nightly occurrence, she became more and more resolved to escape.

Although her life thus far had been one of extreme poverty and tragic loss followed by this nightly shameful surrender to her master's will, she was a defiant and determined young woman. She realised that Regan would tire of her one day or worse still, get her with child. Either way her life would regress to utter impoverishment and if an opportunity arose, she'd have to seize it or accept a ruined future.

As her friendship with young Joe developed more and more, she began to share her dream of escape with him and planted the seed in his mind that he could join her.

'Would you run away, Joe. If you got a chance?' she asked him idly one morning.

'Never gave it a thought,' he replied, 'where could you go? They'd surely find you and make you come back for a flogging.'

'If you took a horse in the night, you could get clean away, before they knew it,' suggested Mary.

'No, Mary. If you stole a horse, they might hang you or send you off to the colonies in America. I've heard it's an awful fate. Weeks aboard a prison ship and then, if you survive that, a life of slavery.'

Nonetheless this wild talk of escape played on his mind. He began to picture a life away from the drudgery of the stables with Mary, for in such a short time, she'd captivated his heart.

* * *

Forever on the alert for an opportunity to carry through her grand plan, Mary thought about the purse of money and gold pocket watch that Regan, when he undressed, invariably threw onto a dressing table. She had little knowledge of the worth of these coins, but they seemed to provide a possible means of making her getaway.

By now the month of May was coming to an end and the changeable weather had settled into proper summer warmth.

Regan summoned her to his bedchamber but seemed to be even more drunk than usual, staggering and reeling all over the room before finally collapsing on the bed. He hadn't tried to molest her at all and almost immediately fell into a deep slumber.

* * *

She waited a little to make sure he was properly asleep. His deafening snores soon convinced her that she'd never have a better chance.

She tiptoed from the room to the outer chamber, gathered the purse of coins and the watch and slipped silently down the stairs and out of the servant's quarters.

On the kitchen table where they all shared their food, there was a batch of fresh bread for the morning. Grabbing a whole loaf, she slipped silently from the building and swiftly crossed the courtyard to the stables.

She knew that Joe slept in an empty stall and went in to him. Shaking him from his slumbers she whispered fiercely. 'Wake up Joe. Come on, stir yourself quickly.'

She showed him her haul of coins and the watch and spoke, with a note of triumph in her voice.

'I've done it now, Joe. There's no turning back for me. Are you going to come too?'

'Oh, Jesus,' groaned Joe, still only half awake. 'If they catch us, it'll be a gallows for us both.'

'Listen,' she urged, 'tis just after midnight. The drunken sot won't wake for hours. Get us a horse and we can have six or seven hours start on him and his men. We can ride north to Dublin. It surely won't be more than two- or three-days ride away.'

'Oh Mary, I don't think it's a good idea,' said Joe, plaintively.

'All right, I'll do it on my own then,' said Mary in defiance. 'I'm not going back now.'

Young Joe had become infatuated with Mary in the few weeks he'd known her. He couldn't bear the thought of her leaving him behind and so he rose and dressed quickly, filling his pockets with his scant belongings - his pocketknife, some hard cheese and a few coins given to him by Regan and his friends as tips.

He supposed that if a hangman's rope was what he'd be facing, he might as well make it worthwhile, so he went to Prince's stall and slipped a bridle over the horse's noble head. Stroking him and whispering to keep him calm, he led him away from the yard hoping the clip clop of his hooves would not disturb the household.

* * *

When they had got well away from the castle and into the woods beyond, he jumped up on Prince's back and pulled Mary up behind him.

They set off in a north-easterly direction across fields and moorland heading for the road which ran between Wexford and Dublin. It had recently been improved greatly and made into a turnpike

It was a fine though moonless night and Joe was loath to set the horse at a gallop for fear of striking a pothole or other obstacle.

* * *

In the kitchen at the castle, a middle-aged woman sat sobbing at the table. She'd guessed that Mary might try something like this, and she'd been woken from her restless slumbers and saw Mary cross to the stable.

She'd wondered whether to go after her and try to stop her but realised that the girl's desperation would brook no argument. When she saw Joe leading the horse across the yard her heart sank even further, for she guessed that he intended to go with her, and that their destiny was something she was helpless to alter.

Elidh's tears were bitter for she had been given no chance to say goodbye, not to a young brother in Joseph Molloy, but as only she and a handful of the senior domestics knew, to her one and only precious son.

Chapter Five

In the very early hours of the next morning, Sam was shaken awake from his deep sleep by Matt.

'Up you get lad or ye'll miss your grub,' he said cheerily.

Sam dressed and hurried, shivering in the cool of the dawn. He crossed the yard to the food hut where a welcoming smell of hot porridge aroused his taste buds.

One of the good things he was finding about his new life was that although the food was plain and monotonous, there was always plenty of it and he gladly accepted the extra dollop and spoonful of jam that one of the ladies heaped on to his platter. There was hot sweet tea too and so Sam was soon replete and ready to face another day's hard grind.

He also observed that the hub of buildings was a lot bigger than he'd first thought and was, in fact, a hive of industry. A carpenter's shop with a huge stack of beams and planks, blacksmiths forge and a kiln for brick making were the most obvious, but the whole place was vast. Horse drawn carts were already being loaded with bricks from a stack of mountainous proportions, ready to be taken along the towpath towards the dig.

The gang marched back to the place where they'd finished the previous day at a good pace, and Sam noticed that the puddling he'd seen being applied last night had already set into the base and sides of the trench.

The foreman George Medlock walked beside Sam and explained some of the detail.

'Sithee yon puddling, lad,' he said. 'They'll be putting another layer down today, and when it's gone off, that bit of the cut will be ready for filling with water.'

'You've the pleasure of that task to come,' he added with a chuckle. 'We tek it in turns at all the different jobs. 'Tis the fairest way.'

When they reached the place where they'd finished the previous night, Sam saw that they were getting closer and closer to a low hill which lay across the planned route.

'What happens when we reach there?' enquired Sam.

'That's where it gets tricky,' replied Medlock. 'We're going to sink shafts down from the top of yon hill and make a tunnel. This morning we should get close to foot of t' hill, and then I'll show thee what your task will be for t' afternoon.'

Soon the sweating, cussing men, including Sam, were getting stuck into the digging just as they had on the previous day. The briny solution had hardened his hands a little and he began digging, determined to pull his weight and give the foreman no reason to doubt his stamina.

Mid-morning, the sky darkened, and a prolonged spell of heavy rain began. At first, they worked through it but as they got more and more soaked, it became impossible to stand, let alone dig, and scores of men scrambled up the hill to where some canvas sheltering had been hastily erected.

After an hour or so the rain relented, and the warm spring sunshine returned.

'We'll get no more done at dig, 'til it dries a bit,' George told his men. 'So, we'll make a start on a shaft for t' tunnel.'

The course of the canal had been marked out with pegs over the crest of the hill, and George's gang were ordered to start digging at a spot where a circle of rope had been laid between the markers. There were four further such circles roughly three hundred yards apart stretching out over the low hill.

Before the first of the circles a curious contraption called a horse gin was being erected by the carpenters. It consisted of a wooden circular reel some seven feet in diameter which was mounted on a pivot ten feet above the ground. A wooden frame surrounded the device, and another one was erected beyond the rope circle.

There was only room for two men to work within the circle, so Jack Willett and Matt took the first turn while the rest of the gang loaded the spoil from the hole onto a horse drawn cart to be taken away. As the hole began to get deeper so the wooden contraption became of use.

A rope was wound tightly around the drum which was fed through to the other frame with pulleys. A huge wooden bucket was attached to this rope line and as the hole got deeper and deeper, so the bucket was positioned and lowered a little way into the hole. The diggers filled it with spoil and rock. Once it was full the bucket was hauled up to the surface by two blinkered horses being led in a circle around the pivot. The other members of the gang were kept busy unloading the spoil and also bricks from a cart that had been brought along the path from the kiln back at the compound.

After an hour or so, the digging team climbed into the bucket and were hauled out of the hole, which was already over five feet deep, to be replaced by Tom and young Sam.

It was hot and exhausting toil, made more tiresome by the confined space in which they were digging. They found it was easier to take turns with the pick and shovel to keep out of each other's way. An hour seemed like eternity but eventually to Sam's great relief Medlock's booming voice told them to get into the bucket for the climb back to the surface.

'Reet, we can do no more here until the brickies have started to line th' hole,' he said, 'so it's back to bottom of th' hill, now.'

Sam was beginning to understand how vast and complex was the undertaking he was part of. On top of the hill, other gangs were starting on the other shafts and another big rope drum machine was being assembled. The sun had already begun to dry the dig and so they were able to put in another couple of hours until the welcome sound of Medlock's whistle brought the day's work to a close.

* * *

Mary, who'd never been up on a horse before, was clinging on to Joe's back for dear life. Her hips and buttocks were feeling very stiff already, but the exhilaration of being free was ample compensation.

After a couple of hours at no more than a slow trot, the dawn was already beginning to break, and Joe was able to give Prince his head and make better progress.

They could do no more than hope that they were heading north and occasional glimpses of the sea on their right hand seemed to confirm this.

They crossed the Slaney River with some trepidation, for although the water level only reached Prince's knees a stumble might have pitched them into the fast-flowing current. Thankfully, it was only a few yards wide at this point and the escapees were much relieved when Prince scrambled up the low bank on the other side.

They prayed that the hours of darkness had given them a precious lead on the search party that would inevitably be coming after them. They realised it would be wise to lie low during daylight hours and to resume their flight by night. They tried to keep the turnpike road in sight without venturing too close to it.

* * *

When the full daylight was upon the land, they found an abandoned hovel - just one of many in that impover-ished countryside.

Joe tethered the horse behind the ruined cottage, trying to keep him out of sight. Providently there was good grazing for him and a small stream close by. Mary took out the bread she'd purloined from the kitchen and along with a piece of Joe's hard cheese, they made a makeshift break-fast that they devoured ravenously. They made themselves as comfortable as possible in the ruins of a poor peasant family's former dwelling.

* * *

Regan awoke in fitful stages, drifting back off several times before finally lifting his head from the pillow and rousing himself. The previous night's roistering with some of his peers had left him distinctly hungover.

The morning was well advanced when he finally rang the bell to summon Mary to attend his needs.

Some minutes elapsed until, to his surprise, it was Mrs Molloy who came into the chamber.

'Where's the girl?' he enquired, brusquely.

'Sir,' she gasped, feigning great surprise, 'the lass is nowhere to be seen.'

'What do you mean, woman,' he grunted, 'she must be somewhere around.'

'No sir, we've searched the whole castle and there's no sight of her anywhere.'

Still in his nightgown, Regan strode into his dressing room.

Immediately he noticed the missing items from the dressing table. 'I might have known it,' he rasped, 'the thieving little whore has run off with my watch and money. By Jesus, she'll rue the day when I get my hands on her. Someone must have helped her; she wouldn't have the nerve to do it alone.'

He glared at the unfortunate Elidh, and seizing her by the shoulders, he continued, 'Was it you, woman? By God I've a mind to have you horse-whipped and thrown out.'

'No sir,' cried Elidh, 'I swear I knew nothing of it.'

'I'll get to the bottom of it, so help me,' he raged. 'I'll put the lot of you good for nothing riff-raff on to the road.'

He continued in similar vein until his wrath subsided somewhat. Elidh tried to shrink into the background, fearing that he would somehow browbeat the truth out of her.

As his initial fury subsided somewhat, he said in a calmer tone, 'She can't have got very far. Right woman, I'll accuse ye no more, but I want the whole staff assembled at once in the main hall.'

So, the entire work force lined up to face the full vent of his fury. It was quite some time before everyone assembled. Male and female domestic staff were quickly gathered in the entrance hall, but by the time the gardeners and other outside workers joined them, almost an hour had passed. All in all, more than sixty lowly people, trembling with dread.

Despite their fear, no-one could spread any light on the mystery, so Regan ordered them all to search high and low for any sign of the missing girl.

Within half an hour, Dan, one of the backward stable lads was brought, shaking with trepidation, to face his master.

'Well, boy,' Regan thundered, 'what do you know of this?'

The poor simple boy could only stammer incoherently, words that Regan couldn't decipher.

'For God's sake will somebody tell me what this imbecile is trying to say, or do I have to beat it out of him?' roared Regan.

A footman, Liam, took a deep breath and blurted out, 'Please sir, he says Joe Molloy can't be found and nor can Prince.'

Regan's face turned puce with rage and he belaboured Dan about the head and shoulders. As the lad began to run, he planted his boot on his rump and left him sprawling.

'Get him out of my sight!' he shouted, 'before I kill the bastard.'

He stood shaking with rage for some minutes, striving to collect his thoughts and come to terms with the fact that not only the girl had fled, but also young Joe and Prince, his pride and joy.

'Mrs Molloy,' he said, at length in a much quieter voice, 'send for Delaney at once and tell him to ensure the constable from the town also attends me.'

Much to the relief of his cowed workforce, he turned on his heel and retired to his chambers.

It was almost noon before Delaney arrived with Sean McClure the constable. Delaney had to ride as far as the larger town of Wexford where McClure was based.

Regan's wrath had cooled to the extent where calm reasoning was possible.

'Right, men,' he began, 'it's obvious that these two thieving scoundrels are in cahoots. They've taken the best horse I have and must be trying to get as far away as quickly as possible. But which way, that's the big question?'

'I'd wager that they'd try for Dublin,' ventured Delaney.

'Mebbe,' answered Regan, 'but I doubt either of them know anything of Dublin, or the distance involved.'

'It's seventy miles or more,' offered McClure. 'Even with a good horse beneath them it's at least three days of hard travel. What with footpads and highwaymen to deal with, I doubt it'll be too long before they come to grief.'

'We'll assume you're right, McClure,' said Regan. 'Assemble a party of good men with the best horses you can muster. Offer them a shilling a day and a crown each when they find them. I want them back here in one piece, mind. We'll assume they got away under the cover of darkness which gives them at least half a day's head start.'

By the time McClure had formed his squad of seven men in the town, selecting only those he knew could handle a horse well, it was already early evening. They rode back to the castle as the daylight was beginning to fade.

Regan was pacing up and down on the courtyard fuming with impatience. 'My God, McClure,' he snarled, 'you've been an age when you know time's a' wasting.'

'I apologise for the delay, sir,' replied McClure, 'in Wexford, it's hard to find suitable horses and men capable of hard riding.'

'Well just get started, every minute is precious.'

Henry the junior footman, acting with an astuteness belying his lowly stature, had searched the stable yard and surrounding parkland and made an interesting discovery.

He approached Regan and excitedly called out, 'Please Sir. I found something.'

'What is it lad,' said Regan, 'it had better be good. I'm in no mood for idiocy.'

'I found hoof-prints in the meadow, sir, leading that way.' He pointed north.

'Show me,' said Regan.

They crossed to the stable yard, and sure enough a discernible trail of hoof prints across the grass towards a copse of trees could be plainly seen.

Regan, although quick to chastise wrongdoing, could also be generous when so inclined and said, 'That's good work Henry my lad, and deserves reward.'

He tossed the lad a shilling from his waistcoat pocket, which the boy caught deftly.

To McClure and his men, he said, 'Well, I'd say that makes it certain which way they went. So off you go McClure. Be sure and bring the thieving madam and the wretch Molloy back to me, alive. I'll have them both on the end of a rope before they're too much older!'

The riders set off at a good canter and rode on until it was becoming difficult to see where they were going.

It was a dark cloudy night unlike the previous one and there was precious little moonlight to help them. One of the horses stumbled over a fallen tree branch and almost threw its rider.

McClure swore softly and ordered his men to slow to a trot.

'It's no good,' he sighed, 'we'll have to make camp until first light.'

They found an abandoned hovel, gathered straw and wood from the remnants of the ruined building, lit a fire and sat around it, passing bottles of poteen and slumbering fitfully.

The conversation centred on the fugitives

'I say good luck to them,' said Fagan. 'Though I think we should have sight of them some time tomorrow.'

'If we do, it'll be God help them,' observed Mahoney. 'Regan'll make sure they swing, just to make an example.'

The talk continued in this vein for some time until one by one they drifted off around the embers of the dying fire.

Chapter Six

The following morning with the weather still in a fickle mood, Medlock's men set off for the dig. A slight overnight frost had left the path treacherous underfoot. Sam almost slipped and would have fallen into the newly dug trench had Mulryan not grabbed his arm.

'Steady does it, boy,' he laughed, ''tis a big drop and we don't want to lose you just yet.'

When they arrived at the work site, Medlock addressed them.

'Right my buckos. This is the plan for the day: we can do no more at shaft until the bricks are laid to line the bit we've already done. That's how it works. We dig a few feet - the brickies line it and then we dig again.'

'How do we know how deep to go?' enquired Tom.

'Ah,' replied Medlock, 'cleverer men than us have surveyed it and worked out that our shaft has to be dug to a depth of eighteen yards.'

'Jesus Christ, that's a long way down towards the devil's door!' said Matt.

'Could be worse,' remarked Medlock, 'next two be even deeper, as t' hill gets higher. In the meantime, we'll make a start at t' foot of yon hill, digging a tunnel that will meet t' shaft eventually.'

So, for the rest of that day Medlock's men and another gang were employed on making a preliminary entrance at the base of the hill. The next day, Friday, work proper began on the entrance to the tunnel. The men joined forces with another gang and made a starter hole in the side of the hill. It was necessary for the earth to be loosened, so shot holes were drilled by hand auger, into which gunpowder was packed, and a further trail laid as a fuse. Medlock blew his whistle and the men hurried well back along the dig while the fuse was lit.

There was a flash and a mighty explosion. A huge amount of rocks and spoil were thrown into the air. When the dust had settled and the smoke cleared, Medlock addressed his gang.

'Reet, lads,' he said, 'start clearing all this rubble. All big rocks you can separate out for use elsewhere.'

All day long they toiled under the hot sun and, when at last Medlock called a halt, the workers had made a sizeable cavity into the hill.

As they made their weary way back to the camp, Medlock told Sam, 'Tomorrow is pay day lad, and a half day. Sunday is your day of rest. The brickies will have finished top of shaft so in t' morning we'll dig down a bit further, and then you get thy wages from Mr Davies.'

* * *

The two young fugitives lay down in the ruins of the hovel and tried to get some sleep, but it was a restless dozing rather than a deep slumber. The enormity of what they'd done weighed heavily on their minds. They knew there could be no turning back to face a grisly reckoning.

After just a couple of hours of this patchy catnapping they were both wide awake, alert for any sound that might herald the approach of their pursuers.

Joe began foraging around for something to eat and hit on a stroke of luck.

The hovel must have been hastily abandoned - the poor inhabitants, probably turned out for failing to pay the rent. Joe found a mound of earth topped with turf and scraping back the soil found a few potatoes. They were rather maggoty and black, but to the young escapees it seemed like a grand feast.

In his solitary life as a stable lad Joe had picked up various wood-crafting skills, one of which was to create fire just by rubbing two dry sticks together.

He gathered some dry grass and twigs and made a small heap. Then with infinite patience, he took two twigs and rubbed them together. It took quite a while, but eventually they started to smoulder and his makeshift blaze got under way.

He cut away the worst of the decay from two large sized potatoes and laid them on the fire, turning them every few moments, until he was satisfied that they were cooked.

They fell on their breakfast voraciously and never was a simple repast more enjoyed.

Joe stamped out the fire immediately afterwards lest the smoke might be seen.

'It's no use waiting for the light to fade, Mary. We'll have to move on,' he said, 'they'll be after us already. We don't know how far behind us, so we'll have to try and keep out of sight.'

So off they set at a steady canter, keeping a wary eye out for anyone who might see them and report them to the chasers who were surely coming behind. They'd managed to salvage a few more of the potatoes which Mary had stowed away inside her bodice.

On they rode, past several small towns and villages, steering well clear. Only the occasional sight of the sea gave them heart that they were still heading north. They made good progress and as the dusk descended, they hoped to find somewhere similar to their previous abode to spend the night. By this time, they were riding through some bleak and desolate country with nary a dwelling place to be seen. It was a beautiful clear evening, and the moon gave an eerie glow to the barren landscape.

The long hours on horseback were proving an arduous undertaking. Mary was much relieved when eventually they came to a small thicket and decided to make this their resting place. There was a small natural pool in a clearing between the trees and both they and the horse drank gratefully from it. Once again Joe used his skill to start a small fire and they ate the rest of the potatoes, saving a couple for the faithful Prince.

The late spring darkness soon gave way to yet another beautiful sunrise, and the weary young fugitives were on their way again. There was no food left and they could only pray that they were nearing their destination, although they had no notion of what to do if they ever got there. They just kept relentlessly on, blessing the faithful horse who never faltered.

Their pursuers had no way of knowing if their quarry would soon be sighted. All the previous day they had ridden hard towards Dublin past the small towns of Gorey and Arklow, where their enquiries bore no information whatsoever. No-one had seen hide nor hair of the missing felons.

They rested for the night near the town of Wicklow within sight of the Wicklow hills and little knew they were but three or four miles east of where Mary and Joe were camped.

* * *

Mary and Joe were desperately hungry. Maggoty potatoes, however welcome at the time, did little to quell their increasing hunger pangs. The range of hills loomed above them on their left and gradually the terrain became a little less forbidding. Small farmsteads were dotted about, and they decided to risk being seen and approach one of these dwellings to beg for food.

An elderly man, stooped and grey with years of toil, eyed them up and down with suspicion.

'Please sir,' entreated Mary, 'we're on our way to Dublin, and we've not eaten in two days. Can ye spare a little food?'

''Tis a fine horse ye have for beggars,' he observed. 'But I'm a man who minds his own business. We have little enough for ourselves. We have nothing to share.'

Mary drew aside and took a coin from her bodice, careful not to let the man see how much she had.

'Look', she said, 'won't you take this for your trouble?'

The man took the coin and examined it closely.

There was something about the young couple's obvious plight and the way she had offered a coin, the worth of which he'd never seen before in his life, that made the old farmer relent.

'Follow me,' he said, leading them towards the cottage.

'Nell,' he shouted to his wife who stood observing them from the doorway, 'give these pair of young scoundrels a plate of pottage, and we'll send them on their way.'

The old lady took them into the cottage and bade them to sit at a rough wooden table on the two stools that seemed to be the only furniture. She served them two platters of a thin watery gruel with some bits of turnip floating around in it and a hunk of hard bread. To the hungry pair it was like manna from Heaven.

'God bless you both,' said Mary, 'is it far to Dublin from here?'

'Ach, I'd say you're still a day's ride away, even with that handsome horse,' said the old man. 'I'd keep away from the turnpike and take the by-ways. You'll probably come across some tinkers on the way.'

'Are they to be feared?' asked Joe.

'Some are honest enough,' answered the old man, 'but they'll try to take that fine steed from you, I'd say, so keep your wits about you.'

The old couple gave them a little hay for Prince and another hunk of the stale bread, and the young adventurers were soon on their way again.

Their pursuers realised that their assumption that the fugitives would try for Dublin using the turnpike was a false one. After two days of fruitless endeavour, they decided on a different strategy and began to course inland.

This change of tactic eventually brought some reward, for after enquiring at several of the small farms scattered among the lower slopes of the Wicklow mountains they came to the very place where the runaways had been given food.

By this time, it was mid-afternoon, and McClure wasted no time on pleasantries.

He addressed the old couple, 'We are in pursuit of two thieves, a lass and a lad on a chestnut horse.'

He could tell immediately from their panic-stricken reaction that the old couple knew of whom he spoke.

'Come on now. I can tell that you know the pair I'm talking of. We have no time for evasion. Tell us what you know, and all will be well.'

'Ay, they came here a' begging this very morn', said the old man, 'but we sent them packing.'

'Which way did they take?'

'They went to the north.'

'Ah, so it must be Dublin. What time would ye say that was?'

'Twas early morn not long after sunrise,' said the old man.

'Thank you, my good sir,' said McClure and threw him a coin.

The old peasant couldn't believe his luck to be rewarded with silver twice in one day - more money than he'd ever seen in his whole life.

'Right, men,' MClure called to his companions, 'we must ride like the wind to catch them.'

They set off at a gallop across the floor of the valley with new purpose.

Meanwhile, Mary and Joe had reached the top of a steep escarpment. They whooped with joy, for below them, albeit still a long way off, the spires and steeples of the second city of the Empire were displayed in all their glory.

Chapter Seven

To Sam, the Saturday morning seemed never ending. The excavation of the shaft continued. The Docherty brothers took the first turn in the chamber, whilst Sam and Mulryan loaded the carts. Medlock, Jack Willett and members of another gang were still tidying the tunnel entrance at the bottom of the hill.

At last, the sound of Medlock's whistle brought a welcome end to the morning's toil.

The workmen all made their way back to the junction with a spring in their step and an air of expectancy. The long week of digging was at an end and their labours were about to be rewarded.

They formed a long line - seventy-four in total. Carpenters, bricklayers, stonemasons and general labourers all shuffled forward to receive their wages.

When Sam's turn came, he was perplexed to receive only six shillings. He'd worked for four and a half days and so was expecting nine shillings. His mystified expression caused Mr Davies to explain, 'Now lad, I've deducted a bob for your boots, as I told you, and two more for your food and ale. You surely didn't expect us to feed you for nothing?'

'No that be right sir,' said Sam respectfully. 'Would you be able to hold it for me 'til I get a chance to go home?'

'Ay, lad, I'll gladly do that for you,' said Davies. 'It'll be Whitsuntide in two weeks and ye'll get an extra day off. Maybe we can get you back home. I'll see what we can do.'

The festive mood among all the men was infectious.

There appeared to be a veritable army of women, that Sam hadn't realised existed, and they seemed to be an integral part of the operation. Although a few of them were the wives and companions of some of the workers, the majority had been recruited from the surrounding parishes to undertake a massive weekly task. They had heated up prodigious amounts of hot water. The week's grime and sweat were washed away with lye soap - an operation that took all afternoon for the whole workforce. Their soiled clothing was removed and laundered in vast wooden tubs, and clean smocks and undergarments issued from a huge pile. All in all, an impressive undertaking, which demonstrated the efficiency and ambition of the Company.

A huge feast awaited the men too. In addition to the usual vegetable broth, four pigs were roasting on a spit at the back of the eating hut, filling the whole campsite with a delicious aroma.

Sam queued patiently and was eventually rewarded with a platter piled high with roast pork and potatoes. Cider, ale and gin were also provided in abundance.

The reason for all this largesse was quite simple. The company's agents had been sharply criticised for allowing the workforce to run riot through the surrounding villages, looting, molesting the womenfolk, and generally terror-ising the local populace. The claims for compensation were huge, and the agents quickly came up with an ideal compromise solution. By supplying the men with this lavish hospitality, it was hoped to keep them on site. It seemed to be working well, for every weekend became an occasion of great revelry.

The only downside was in the alcohol fuelled brawling that was commonplace, although it was never serious enough to cause more than a few sore knuckles, cuts and bruises.

Sam joined in the fun and games, albeit with some hesitation. His upbringing in a God-fearing household had left him completely unused to hard drinking or roistering, but he was soon entering into the spirit of things and became quite drunk in a short space of time.

Someone produced a battered old fiddle from some-where and another a penny whistle, and the party took on another dimension. Singing bawdy old songs and shanties, twirling the women round in a series of jigs and reels, the hard-working men partied well past the dusk and into the night.

Sam staggered drunkenly to his palliasse and fell fast asleep, completely overwhelmed by the experiences of his first week's work on the mighty project.

Chapter Eight

Still keeping well hidden in a small spinney halfway down the steep hillside, Mary and Joe spent an uncomfortable night huddled together. The end of their arduous flight for freedom was almost in sight, although they had no idea of what to do or where to seek shelter when they reached the great metropolis. Their proximity to one another induced an inevitable stirring of desire in Joe's loins, but he was so in awe of the comely lass sleeping soundly at his side. Mindful of what she must have suffered at the hands of Fintan Regan, he had no wish to sully the feeling of companionship that was growing between them, and so kept his adolescent desires under firm control.

At first light they began to descend the cart track that led into the valley below. Ahead of them they noticed a plume of smoke rising high into the still air.

Mindful of what the old man had told them about the presence of gypsies, they tried to find a way to avoid confrontation, but it was to prove to be impossible. The only path down the rocky hillside was the one they were on, and soon they found themselves travelling through a gathering of caravans parked by the side of the track.

A small crowd of curious people, mostly children, emerged from the caravans.

Dogs yapped at Prince's legs, unsettling him. Joe tried to steer the jittery horse cautiously through the throng, but to no avail. A tall olive-skinned man with a vicious looking mastiff on a rope tether stood in their way.

The dog was growling ominously, unsettling the horse still more and it took all Joe's efforts to hold him steady.

'Good morn to ye,' said the man. The politeness of his greeting could not conceal the threat of menace in the air. 'And where might two young spalpeens be off to on such a handsome horse?'

Joe took the initiative and answered boldly, 'We've business in Dublin for our master, so kindly let us pass.'

'Ah so, business, is it?' said the man with an air of intimidation in his voice. 'It'd be a foolish master that entrusted his affairs to a lass and a gossoon.'

The dog began to bark ferociously and suddenly lunged at the horse.

Joe shouted, 'Hold on tight to me, Mary.'

He gave the horse his head and kicked his heels against its hind quarters, whilst Mary clung tightly to him.

Prince needed no second bidding and shot forward. The gypsy man dived out of the way at the last second, and they ran the gauntlet to a chorus of imprecations and a fusillade of stones fired at them. A big boulder caught Mary a glancing blow on the shoulder, almost dislodging her, but she managed to keep hold of Joe's waist and they galloped down the track at breakneck speed. Mary was in mortal fear of Prince losing his footing and throwing them. After a hair-raising ten minutes or so, Joe managed to rein the horse in. They'd left the gypsy camp far behind, but the danger was not over.

Looking around they saw to their dismay and consternation that a group of three or four of the gypsy men had mounted their horses and were in pursuit.

Two of the chasers went off at a tangent trying to get ahead and cut them off. For an hour or more a deadly game of cat and mouse ensued, but the gypsy's ill-used and neglected ponies were no match for the thoroughbred Prince and the expertise of his rider. Giving him his head again, Joe gradually edged away from his pursuers. Eventually they realised the futility of their quest and gave it up, hurling yet more abuse at their elusive quarry.

It had been a close and threatening encounter, but mercifully it was to prove the only one, and they were able to continue at a far more comfortable pace.

At around midday they stopped by a fast-flowing brook to let Prince take a drink. The gallant steed had taken them almost seventy miles in under four days, but he was showing signs of distress, his flanks foaming with sweat. Joe splashed him with water from the stream and let him nibble at the abundant green grass by the side of the track. Although they were sore and aching and desperately hungry, they knew that maybe another hour or two would see them arrive at the great metropolis.

'Well, Joe,' she said, rubbing her bruised shoulder, 'thank God, I think we've made it, but what are we going to do next?'

'I don't know, Mary, we need to plan. I reckon it's a big place and maybe we can just lose ourselves for a while.'

'Regan won't give up looking for us,' she said. 'I heard somewhere that ships for England sail from here. Maybe we could try to get on one of those.'

'That won't be easy to do,' replied Joe.

'No, I know that, but the longer we stay around here, the more chance of getting caught. We've come this far, we're not going to give up now.'

She counted out the money she had snatched - she knew nothing of its value or what use it would be. The watch must be worth a quite a lot, but again she had no idea of how to raise money for it.

'Do you think we have enough to buy passage on a ship?' she asked.

'I really don't know,' answered Joe, 'we'll just have to try and find out.'

'What'll we do with the horse, Joe?'

'Reckon we'll try to sell him,' he answered, 'or just turn him loose.'

'Wouldn't seem right to just leave him. He's been our saviour; we'll have to try and find him a good owner,' said Mary.

They mounted up again and before long the track joined the turnpike, and they had no choice but to take it for the last leg of the journey. The road was busy with wagons and carts, laden with produce.

They drew closer to the city and were relieved that none of their fellow travellers paid them any heed. Having paid a twopenny fee at the toll house, in the early evening they reached the outskirts of the capital.

The elegance of the fine tall buildings and the sheer number of people thronging the wide streets were overwhelming to the youngsters. Carriages full of elegant ladies and dandies mingled with carts that seemed to criss-cross at junctions in a haphazard fashion. It was a bewildering and anxious experience.

They gazed open mouthed with wonder at the spectacle. As they progressed nearer to the city centre the traffic grew even heavier, unsettling their hero Prince who, like them, had never been in such a strange and noisy environment. They dismounted and led the horse along a wide boulevard of imposing mansions.

On the opposite side of this grand street stood a terrace of shops offering all manner of goods - fine clothing and boots on display, and then an apothecary offering a bewildering display of potions and bottles. Further along, the smell of food emanating from a pie shop made them almost faint with hunger.

'We have to eat Joe,' said Mary, 'let's get something each from yon shop.'

Joe, who had more experience of coinage than Mary, selected a silver sixpence and went over to the shop, and purchased two large crusty pies filled with meat and potatoes. In a small side street. Joe tethered Prince to a tree which they squatted beneath, and they devoured the pies with great gusto.

'I think we need to get somewhere near the harbour,' said Joe.

'What about Prince?' asked Mary. 'We can't just set him loose – we'll keep him until something turns up.'

'Yes, of course,' replied Joe, 'we'll just lead him, though. All this noise and bustle is unsettling him.'

They set off on foot for what they hoped was the right direction. The road they were walking along ran adjacent to a wide river, which they hoped with any luck would bring them to the dock area.

As they travelled, the streets began to get meaner and less well maintained. Children in rags played in the muddy streets beneath grim tenement buildings. They sensed an air of menace in the atmosphere. Mary felt as if many eyes were watching them, and she shivered with trepidation.

'Let's try to find lodging for the night,' Joe. 'Surely we'll have enough money for that.'

They kept walking a while longer and dusk was falling when at last, they came to a quayside where several tall ships were moored.

Even this late in the day it was a scene of bustling activity. Men were wheeling sacks, barrels and barrow loads of all kinds of merchandise up gang planks and onto the decks. The quayside was a wide concourse bordered by a row of buildings. All manner of people were scurrying to and fro, between chandlers' stores, and warehouses. A little further along, and to their great relief, they found a livery stable full of horses in a row of stalls.

They approached a man who seemed to be presiding over the activities of various stable hands. Some were sweeping the cobbled yard, others filling mangers with fresh hay.

'What can I do for you?' said the man. He was quite short in stature but had an air of authority about him that seemed to brook no shilly-shallying.

'State your business. I'm a busy man,' he said abruptly.

'We want to sell our horse; would you make us an offer?' asked Joe meekly.

The man approached them and looked the horse up and down.

'Well, he's a noble looking fellow, right enough,' he said, 'and would make a fine stallion at stud, but I doubt he's yours to sell at all. I dare say you must have stolen him.'

The couple looked at each other, lost for a plausible explanation, until Mary suddenly took the initiative.

'Please sir, won't you help us. We escaped from a cruel master and have been on the roads for many a day. No-one knows we came this way. We no longer need the horse but want him to be well cared for.'

The man made a careful examination of Prince while he was contemplating their plea.

After a few anxious moments for them, he announced his decision. 'This is how I see it. You've obviously stolen this animal and I should denounce you and confiscate it, but you seem genuine enough. So, I'm inclined to take a chance and help you out. I'll give you three guineas and no more questions asked.'

Noticing Joe's crestfallen face, he added, 'Look lad, I know the horse is worth much more than that. But I'm taking a mighty gamble that nobody's going to come looking for a while. That's my offer. Take it or leave it.'

'We'll take it, sir, and thank you,' said Mary, before Joe had a chance to object.

The horse trader gave the three gold coins to Mary, and Joe handed over Prince with tears tripping unashamedly down his cheeks. The gallant animal had given them their chance of freedom, and the parting from him was so hard for the young lad to bear.

'Come on, Joe,' said Mary in an effort to console him. 'We can't take him with us, and this man will give him a good life, won't you sir?'

'Ay, don't fret, lad,' said the man patting Joe on the arm. 'He'll come to no harm here.'

With that, Mary pulled a still sobbing Joe away and they went a little further along the quay side to a large tavern with a sign swinging from a beam that proclaimed it was the Duke of Leinster Inn.

Hesitantly they went inside. They fought their way through a jostling, noisy throng of drinkers to a long counter and managed to catch the eye of a large lady who was serving tankards of beer to her thirsty customers. She eyed them with a certain air of suspicion.

'What can I get you?' she asked Joe.

Mary adopted the same role of spokesperson that she had at the stables and answered the woman herself.

'My husband and I want lodging for the night if you have it.'

'Oh, do you now,' retorted the woman. She continued to peer at the young couple with distrust. 'You seem very young to be wed, and I see no ring on your finger. This is no bawdy house, I'll have you know.'

Mary, acting with her newfound decisiveness that was growing by the minute, threw down one of the guinea coins on to the counter.

'We were married this very morn, and we had no time to buy a ring,' she said, 'surely this will cover the cost of your best room?'

The woman picked up the coin, shrugged her shoulders and said, 'Follow me.'

She lit a candle and led them up a rickety staircase along a passage with several doors leading off it. She opened one of the doors to reveal a room with a large, canopied bed with linen of somewhat grubby appearance A table with a large bowl and jug of water was the only other furnishing. She lit another candle and placed it on the table.

'You can stay here for tonight, but I want you out in the morning. Married indeed,' she scoffed.

The young couple just removed their boots and outer garments and despite the dubious quality of the bed clothes, they snuggled close to one another and exhausted beyond measure, rapidly fell asleep.

Chapter Nine

Sam awoke, feeling rather fuzzy, and staggered out of the tent. He'd never consumed so much alcohol in his life. He made his way over to the water butts and poured a pitcher of water over his head. The shock of the cold water swiftly revived him. The smell of frying ham from the communal area made him acutely aware of his ravenous hunger. A few of his workmates were already breakfasting and one of the ladies handed him a platter of ham and eggs.

He noticed that George Medlock was sitting on his own. He approached cautiously and said, 'Can I join you, sir?'

'Ay lad, thou can. No need to call me sir, Mr Medlock or gaffer will be fine. Well, that's thy first week under thy belt, and I'm well pleased with ye.'

'I hope I've pulled my weight,' said Sam. 'It's hard going but I'm going to stick at it.'

'Well lad there's work here for years to come if ye want it. I've heard that the big businessmen have in mind a network stretching the length and breadth of the whole land. Men like us will allus have a job.'

He continued, 'As we're diggin' yon tunnel, other gangs are working their way up toward us from as far south as the Trent. Times are a' changing boy, and who knows where it will all end.'

When they'd finished eating, Medlock invited Sam to take a walk to nearby Preston on the Hill.

'Is there a church or chapel there?' enquired Sam.

'Not that I know of,' George answered. 'Why, is that important to you?'

'Don't suppose it is really,' replied Sam. 'It's just the way I've been brought up.'

'Never had much truck with religion, mysen,' said George, 'just try and do what's reet by folk and ye'll not go far wrong.'

They reached a long field with a swiftly flowing brook running through the middle.

'Hang on a while gaffer,' said Sam.

He found some stout twigs by the brook and, taking some twine he'd scrounged from the store, he quickly fashioned a couple of snares and placed them under the hedgerow.

'Didn't know you were a poacher, lad,' chuckled George, 'tha lives and learns.'

'Ay, my Uncle Cedric showed me how,' replied Sam. 'I'm already missing my mother's rabbit stew. I wonder if the ladies could put a couple of fat bucks to good use?'

'I'm sure that'd go down reet well with t' lads,' said George.

'I'll come back tonight to see if I've had any luck,' said Sam.

They continued towards the village, following the course of the stream.

'I reckon they'll use this stream and others to fill t' cut,' remarked George. 'Thou'll see then what all t' diggings been for then.'

Sam felt completely at ease in the company of the older man and began to ply him with questions

'Have you been a long time in the canal business, then?' he asked.

'About three or four years, give or take, I'd say.'

'What did you do before that?' asked Sam.

'Well, when I were a lad of your age I was apprenticed to a millwright near 'Uddersfield. Learned all about controlling water supply, picked up a bit of joinery and bricklaying. I were doing all reet 'til millwright Hardcastle upped and died of a fever. That were me out of a job. Left ould folk behind and went looking for work, here and there.'

'How did you finish up here though?' asked Sam.

'Well, bit be bit, I drifted towards Manchester and then found mesen at Bridgewater canal. Worked hard and finished up as foreman. You could do same lad if tha keep thy wits about ye.'

'Did you ever meet the famous Mr. Brindley?'

'Ay. I did several times. Rum sort of bloke, but bloody canny - knew what he wanted and how to go about it.'

Soon they arrived back at the compound, where the workers were all enjoying their leisure time. Several card schools were in progress and although the banquet was not as lavish as the previous day, there was still plenty of it.

Sam joined the Docherty brothers and their cousin Gerard, who were just lounging around drinking ale.

He learned how they'd been recruited by an agent back in Donegal. Promises of good wages and plenty of work had been enough to persuade them to leave their impoverished villages in droves and in some cases, bringing along their wives and sweethearts. Leaving parents and siblings behind, with promises to return with riches untold, they were transported to Belfast and then across the sea to Liverpool at their employer's expense. Sadly, and perhaps inevitably, those good intentions were soon forgotten in all but the most prudent of them. It was far too easy after a week's hard graft to spend their wages on drinking and gambling. Loved ones over the sea were easily forgotten - such is human nature.

* * *

On the Monday morning and with many a sore head, it was back to the dig. The workers split into their various gangs and continued where they'd left off.

For Medlock's men, it was back to the shaft to dig down another few feet. Sam, eager to impress, was first into the bucket, joined by Tom again, and they slogged away for an hour under the warm May sun, filling the bucket several times with rocks and soil. Then it was the turn of Jack and Gerard in the hole, whilst the rest of the gang loaded the carts for hauling away.

After the midday meal break, they were engaged in enlarging the tunnel itself. Once more charges were laid, and a huge mass of rubble was disturbed. By this time, they had made inroads to a distance of more than twenty yards, and candles had to be lit to enable them to work in the almost pitch-black cavern. As they hacked away, Sam's pick caught on a rock and sparks began to fly. One of them ignited an unburned heap of gunpowder. There was an explosion, which although not very powerful, was enough to dislodge more of the boulders, one of which caught Jack Willet heavily.

He shouted out in agony, his left forearm pinned beneath the huge rock. His workmates managed to lift the rock enough to free him, but his lower arm, wrist and hand were in a sorry state.

They helped him from the tunnel, disquieted by his moans of agony, knowing full well that it could have been any one of them. Poor Jack had drawn the short straw.

It took an agonisingly long time to take the injured man back to the compound. Grey faced with pain Willet, could only stagger along at a funereal pace.

No proper medical aid was available, and it was left to the women, including Jack's wife Nell, to wash and dress his wounds as best they could.

Medlock took charge of the situation.

'Reet, men,' he said, 'we've done what we can for Jack, but there's no point in hanging around here moping about it, so we'd best get back to it.'

They had no option but to obey, but it was with heavy hearts and a mood of great apprehension that they walked back to the scene of the disaster.

They went through the motions of completing a day's work, but nobody's heart was really in it, and then they tramped dejectedly back to the camp.

Davies had summoned a surgeon from the village, but there was little he could do for Jack, apart from putting a splint on his shattered wrist.

There were to be many more similar accidents before the mighty undertaking was completed, including several fatalities. Such was the lot of these brave men engaged on this massive enterprise of civil engineering. No insurance or compensation schemes existed, and so the fate of injured workers was down to the goodwill of the various employers. In Willett's case, the Company, in a rare display of compassion, awarded him a payment of five guineas and sent him back to his humble farm dwelling, just a few miles distant.

Chapter Ten

After the adversities of their harrowing flight, Mary and Joe slept solidly and awoke to the sounds of the busy quayside - a cacophony of shouts and cusses of the various dock workers, mingled with the raucous screeching of seagulls.

Mindful of the frosty reception they'd received the night before, they washed and made their toilet as best they could. They ventured down the rickety staircase, hoping to steal out unnoticed.

However, to their surprise, the fearsome landlady met them at the bottom with a completely different approach from the one she'd used the night before.

'I hope ye found the room to your liking for your honeymoon?' she said with a laugh. 'Come now, your payment will stand you a little breakfast afore ye go.'

She bade them sit at a table and put a plate of oatcakes, cheese and sliced onions before them, and also two tankards of the dark stout for which Dublin was already famous.

'I've seen many such as yourselves and heard many a tale of woe,' she said. 'So, I turns a blind eye to most things, but I'd be curious to know what a young pair like youse are going to do in this big evil town of ours. It can swallow ye up in a trice, if you don't keep your wits about ye.'

Mary looked across at Joe and once more decided to put their cards on the table.

The woman seemed friendly - completely different from the fierce crone of the previous night.

'We escaped from a cruel monster of a man who made our lives hell,' she said. 'We're going to try to board a ship for England.'

'Are you indeed. Have ye money to pay your passage?' asked the woman. 'I've heard it's two pounds or more each and not a voyage for the faint-hearted.'

'We don't have much money,' said Mary. 'Also, we don't want to leave any trace behind.'

'Ah, so. I might know of someone who could help ye,' suggested the woman. 'Give me a little time. Go now and discover some of the wonders of Dublin town but be very wary. Come back at nightfall. I might have some news for ye then. If you go astray on your way back, just ask for Winnie Carey at the Duke of Leinster. Everybody knows me!'

So, they took the Mrs. Carey's advice, and retraced their steps back towards the centre, where they'd seen all the magnificent shops.

For the simple country boy and girl every corner they went round brought new amazing sights. They sat for a while by the side of the river just watching the busy city dwellers going about their daily routine.

'Let's count our money out,' said Joe, 'so we know what we have.'

Mary, completely unused to money at all, was happy to let him take charge of their precious little hoard.

Joe carefully counted out the assorted coins.

'We have the two guineas, five gold crowns and eight silver sixpences.'

He used his fingers to tot up the total. 'I reckon that makes three pounds and eleven shillings plus these few coppers.'

'What about the Regan's watch?' Mary asked, 'that must surely be worth a fair sum.'

'Oh, yes, I think it would be,' agreed Joe, 'but I reckon we should hold on to it. If we manage to get across to England, we'll probably be able to sell it there.'

They resumed their ambling along and presently came to street market. A long line of stalls with all manner of goods lined both sides of a busy thoroughfare. A huge crowd of people thronged the street with much shoving and jostling.

'Hold tight to the money Joe,' warned Mary.

'Don't worry I will. You hold my hand in case we lose each other. Never seen so many people in my life.'

Used only to the destitute town of Wexford and its surrounding district, they were awestruck at the plethora of wares on offer. Barrows laden with all kinds of fruit and vegetables, some of which the youngsters had never seen before. Other barrows displayed massive hams and cheeses. Poultry and rabbits trussed up by the feet, along with mountains of pies and loaves of bread. They watched in fascination as a man plunged apples into a vat of a hot sticky substance and put them to cool on a wire tray.

'Toffee apples, tuppence apiece,' he cried.

'Oh, let's have one Joe,' pleaded the excited girl.

Joe handed over a sixpenny piece and, using his newly found fiscal responsibility, had the sense to put out his hand for the two pennies of change.

They crunched through the crispy shell. Mary had never tasted anything so sweet and delicious in her whole life.

All day they roamed through the hustle and bustle of the great metropolis soaking up the atmosphere and for a while managing to put the traumatic experience of the past few days out of mind.

As the light began to fade, they returned to the quayside and the Leinster tavern.

Mrs Carey was waiting for them with a man of twenty years or so. He was a tall spare individual with a sallow complexion and long red hair tied into a pigtail.

'This is Will Potter', she said. 'He can help you, but he has a price.'

'So, I can get you on the Foxhunter, if that's what you want,' he told them. 'She's that big three-master lying just over the way there, and she sails on the full tide at midnight.'

'We've very little money,' said Mary.

'Don't worry about that,' said Potter with a laugh. 'You won't exactly be travellin' in style.'

'What do you mean?' said Joe suspiciously.

Potter laughed, 'Depends if you can stand roughing it a bit.'

'Tell them what you mean, Will,' said Mrs Carey. 'Stop beating about the bush.'

'Right,' continued Potter, 'I can slip you aboard, but you'll be down in the hold hiding behind the barrels and boxes.'

'How long would that be for?' asked Mary.

'Depends on the winds,' said Potter. 'Sometimes it takes three days - sometimes a week or more.'

Mary and Joe exchanged worried glances.

'What would we do for food and drink?' she asked.

'I'd bring you something when I could,' said Potter. 'I'll give you time to think about it, but you need to be by the gang plank by eleven sharp. Oh, by the way it'll be a crown each for my trouble.'

He slipped out of the door and disappeared into the multitude swarming over the quay side loading the three moored ships.

'You'd better come into my kitchen,' said Mrs Carey to Mary, 'I reckon you need some attention.'

They accompanied the landlady into a large kitchen area.

'Sit you down there my lady', she ordered, guiding Mary to a stool.

From a rack of utensils, she selected a fearsome looking pair of shears.

'Right my dear. It's time to lose those lovely locks of yours.'

'Oh no!' gasped Mary. 'Why would I need to do that?'

'Look here,' said Mrs Carey. 'If ye have the bad luck to get caught on board, it'll go a lot better for ye if ye can pass for a lad. Surely, I don't have to say more?'

'No, I understand what you mean,' answered Mary, shyly.

With that, Mrs Carey busied herself snipping away, and Mary's long flowing hair quickly became a thing of the past.

She stood back and admired her handiwork.

'That'll do ye,' she said, 'now I must find you some lad's clothing. Both my boys are away at sea so I should be able to fix you up.'

Half an hour later the transformation was complete, and Joe could hardly believe his eyes. A handsome young man in smock, breeches and cloth cap stood before him.

Mrs Carey's change of demeanour was another minor miracle.

Gone was the forbidding dragon of the previous night. She had become a kindly soul who'd taken the young fugitives to her bosom and couldn't do enough for them.

She gathered a good supply of the oatcake and cheese along with some apples and a flask of water, placed them all in a bundle, and handed it to Joe.

'Ye'll need this,' she said. 'Will Potter can't be relied on too well so this bit of grub should see ye right.'

By this time nightfall had descended and it was time to go.

'How can we ever repay you for your kindness, lady?' asked Mary.

'Ach, don't fret now,' replied the woman. 'I'm just glad to give young 'uns like yourselves a help to escape the accursed mess our masters have made of this country of ours. Good luck and God speed.'

With that she turned on her heel and went back to her thirsty customers.

They stepped out onto the quayside and walked the hundred yards or so to where the Foxhunter was moored, keeping to the shadows.

At first there was no sign of Potter, but then they heard a "Pssst" from the side of a warehouse building just a few feet from where they were standing.

'Over here,' hissed Potter. 'We'll wait for a chance to slip up the gang way. That chance will only come once so wait for me to give a signal, oh and I'll take the two crowns now.'

Joe dutifully handed over the coins, and Potter slipped them into his breeches.

There was a lull in the activity surrounding the vessel, so Potter said 'Right. This is it, follow me.'

They zig-zagged across the cobbles and ran up the long gang plank. Once on the deck, they crouched beside a lifeboat.

When he considered it safe to do so, Potter darted towards the open hold and scrambled down the ladder with the young couple close behind.

The dim light of a few oil lamps was enough for Potter to lead them to a hiding place behind a stack of barrels .

'Right, this'll be your home 'til we get to Liverpool. When we set sail, these lamps will be gone so you'll be in the dark, but I'll come to you whenever I can. Good luck.'

With that he was gone.

By the dim light afforded by the lamps, they were just able to take bearings of their situation. The hold, or so it seemed to the young couple, was a vast cavern with all manner of cargo. Barrels and crates, sacks of grain and, in one corner, stalls containing four horses.

They cautiously explored a little further and discovered a heartening sight. A row of huge water butts - obviously the fresh water supply for the ships company.

They heard the sound of approaching footsteps descending the ladder and stole back to their hiding place. To their great relief they saw it was Will Potter.

'We're just about to cast off,' he whispered. 'I've come to turn the lamps out, so you'll be in the dark. I'll try to come in the morning, but I have to take care, so don't worry if I don't come for a while.'

With that, one by one he extinguished the lanterns, closed the hatch and they were plunged into almost complete darkness.

They felt every shudder and creak as the huge vessel was carried away downstream to the open sea. They clung to one another as each new sound and roll of the ship induced fresh dread into their nervous minds. The squeaking and scurrying of rats added to the nightmare scenario as that first long night at sea went inexorably on.

The rats had scented their bag of oatmeal and cheese, and soon they were overwhelmed by the loathsome creatures crawling all over them to get at it.

In the midst of their desperation, Joe had a brainwave. As their eyes gradually acclimatized to what little light there was, he crawled over to where he remembered the sacks of grain were stored and groping his way to the stack, he split one open with his knife. He grabbed a handful and made a trail of spilt corn back to Mary who was trying to beat the rats away with little success.

It seemed to do the trick and most of the rats soon left to feast on this more attainable food supply. Some of the more persistent of their number were still a problem, and they had no choice but to keep kicking and lashing out with their fists to drive them away.

The abject misery of the voyage was something that they would never forget. They clung to one another in a vain effort to combat the cold. The almost pitch blackness was only alleviated when an occasional visit by crew member to fetch water or feed the horses gave a temporary dim light. Even then, the constant threat of discovery had them rigid with fear.

The attacks by the malevolent vermin seemed interminable and made proper sleep impossible. The thought of giving themselves up and pleading for merciful treatment was growing stronger with each passing hour.

Despite their wretchedness, which seemed would never end, in fact fortune favoured the brave. The Foxhunter was borne all the way across the Irish sea on a stiff westerly breeze in just three days.

In the hold two very frightened, half-starved (for their food had run out after the second day) young people sat clinging to one another in forlorn despondency.

Potter hadn't kept his promise to provide for them, and the constant water supply had been their only salvation.

They sensed that the voyage was coming to an end as the ship was no longer pitching and rolling. They waited on tenterhooks as the Foxhunter was brought alongside the quay, and they heard the shouts of men throwing ropes down to secure her.

When at last the hatch was thrown open, their first glimpse of daylight since they'd left Ireland was almost blinding.

As their eyes gradually adjusted to the brightness they could see and hear deckhands descending the ladder to begin unloading the cargo. Dodging between the barrels and crates, they managed to get to the foot of the ladder undiscovered.

They ascended on to the deck, but then their luck ran out, for as they emerged onto the deck they were spotted.

'Well, well my hearties?' crowed a huge sailor, with a fearsome looking black beard. 'I trust you enjoyed the voyage.'

Turning to three other men of equally menacing status, he went on, 'seems we have found two new deckhands, just what we needed.'

The stowaways were seized by the four men and dragged towards the officer who was supervising the unloading.

'Ah well, and what have we here?' he crowed, 'thought ye could have free passage over the sea, did you my bould boyos?'

'Bring them to the bridge,' he ordered their captors. 'These two wretches are probably the two we were warned to keep a lookout for.'

He examined the two trembling youngsters more diligently. 'I was told it was a lad and a girl,' he mused, 'but that information seems somewhat awry, unless….'

He snatched at Mary's hat.

'Aha,' he crowed triumphantly. 'A very winsome boy indeed! Let's see what the skipper wants to do with them.'

The confrontation was taking place adjacent to the gangplank. Will Potter suddenly appeared, struggling under the weight of the sack of grain on his back. Quickly taking stock of the critical situation, he contrived to buckle at the knees and fell at the feet of the men and their prisoners. They released their grip to go to the aid of the fallen man and Joe, quick as a flash, shouted, 'Run for it, Mary.'

In the confusion, they ran headlong down the gangway and dodging many an outstretched arm or leg, managed to escape immediate capture by running up a labyrinth of alleys and lanes until they were well clear of the quayside.

They realised to their great relief that after a few moments no-one was earnestly giving chase, so they hid themselves in the entrance of a dark alley between two tall buildings to get their breath back. They guessed that Will Potter, despite his broken promise of providing food, had made amends by deliberately creating the diversion that had aided their escape, and they thanked him profoundly in his absence.

In spite of their straitened circumstances, they felt a certain exhilarating sense of freedom. Whatever trials and tribulations lay in front of them, Regan's tyrannical hold over them had been broken and here they were in a strange land with their destinies in their own hands.

If they'd known how close their pursuers had been to catching them, they wouldn't have felt so elated.

McClure and his men had ridden through the gypsy camp a few hours after the young fugitives and ascertained that they had indeed passed by. They joined the turnpike and at the toll house obtained further confirmation.

Locating their quarry in the vast urban sprawl of the capital, however, had proved too great a task.

McClure surmised correctly that they would probably head for the harbour, and so they made a thorough search of the area, questioning all and sundry, but to no avail.

It seemed no trace of them had been seen. McClure had his suspicions that someone must have knowledge of the pair, but despite of visiting all the ships that were currently loading at the quayside no information was to be had.

McClure left instructions all along the dockside to be on the lookout for a lad and girl.

They could do no more, and reluctantly began the long homeward trek to face the wrath of Squire Regan.

* * *

Dusk was beginning to fall, and the youngsters observed that in Liverpool, the district around the dock side was almost a carbon copy of Dublin. Mean streets where poor ragged people went about their business. Surprisingly they could hear many Irish accents among the throng, and even more surprisingly, there were a number of men and women with skin as black as coal.

Desperate as they were for food, they daren't risk going into a tavern or shop for fear of being apprehended.

Costermongers were closing their barrows for the night, and Mary and Joe managed to cadge some rotting apples, a loaf of hard bread and some ham of dubious ancestry.

They slipped inside a derelict warehouse to consume their meagre meal.

As they munched on the food, Mary recalling their narrow escape said, 'When we were hauled before that officer on the ship did you heed what he said?'

'No,' replied Joe, 'I was too scared and looking for a chance to struggle free.'

'He said,' continued Mary, 'that we must be the two they'd been told to look out for. Which means Regan's men must have been closer than we'd hoped.'

'Oh God, so we're not clear yet then,' said Joe, 'not by any means.'

'We've just got to stay low,' said Mary, 'try to dodge from place to place 'til the hue and cry dies down.'

'We'd best not look for lodging, then,' offered Joe. 'We'll have to find shelter where we can. Seems like there's plenty of places like this round here.'

'Can't be any worse than that what we've just been through with all those damned rats,' observed Mary.

So began a few days of tense, nerve-wracking existence for the young couple. They roamed the streets by day, trying to keep themselves to themselves, buying a little food from various barrow men and huddling together in a different warehouse or grain store every night. The weather had been ideal - pleasantly warm and dry for the most part. However, Regan's money, which had seemed like a small fortune at the start, was gradually dwindling away, and they were at their wits end wondering how long they could avoid capture and what the future had in store for them.

Fate took a hand once again, in the form of a large black man who jumped out of the shadows just as they were trying to slip inside a warehouse for the night.

'Hold right there,' he commanded, shining his lantern on them. 'What's your business in here?'

'We're not thieving, sir,' said Mary humbly. 'We're just looking for shelter for the night.'

The man held up the lantern and scrutinised their faces.

'On the run are ye?' he said, and then adopting a friendlier tone added, 'don't worry I'll not turn you in, I've known plenty of that life myself. You'd best come with me.'

'Where to?' asked Joe anxiously.

'Just take my word,' said the man, his black face lit with a friendly beaming smile. 'I'll find you a proper bed for the night and a bit of grub.'

Realising that they had little choice, Mary and Joe followed the man along a dark alleyway and out onto a wider street still thronging with people even at this late hour. A few hundred yards along he turned down a side street and up to the door of a small chapel. He struck the door three times with slow deliberate knocks. After what seemed an interminable wait, the door was opened by a clergyman. They were relieved to see that from his garb he seemed to be a Catholic priest.

'Ah, Reuben,' he addressed the man. 'Yet more waifs and strays, is it?'

''Tis so, Father,' answered Reuben, 'can you help them?'

'Let me have a proper sight of them.' He looked them up and down. 'I suppose the constables are after you, is that so?'

'We've done nothing wrong Father,' pleaded Mary.

'I can tell from your speech that you've come from across the sea,' said the surprisingly young-looking priest. 'You have no need to explain further. We can give you shelter, but only for a short time. Come with me.'

He led them through a door at the side of the altar to a small room with a table and several stools.

'Sit you down and I'll see if I can find you something to eat,' he said, and addressing Reuben added, 'thank you Reuben. You are truly a kind and generous soul, but I hope these are the last for a while.'

'Very well, Father,' answered Reuben. 'I'll do my best not to trouble you further.'

Both Mary and Joe thanked him profusely and their benefactor went back out into the night.

'A truly, good man,' said the priest. 'A freed slave of James Penney and an asset to this parish, employed as a night watchman. He often brings me troubled souls such as yourselves.'

Another door opened and a young girl of about the same age as Mary appeared. The priest bade her to bring food for the fugitives.

'Tis simple fare we take here,' said the priest, 'but you're welcome to share it.'

The maid soon returned with two plates of potatoes and gravy.

He spoke a grace and the hungry pair fell on the first hot food they'd had since they left Dublin over a week previously.

Mary decided to put her trust in the kindly priest and told him the whole story of their flight from Ireland.

He listened intently and when Mary had finished her story, he gave the matter some thought and then said,

'I greatly admire the courage and fortitude you have shown on getting this far, but I think that Liverpool will always be a perilous place for you. If you stay here, it will be only a matter of time before you're discovered and arrested.'

He continued 'You'd be best advised to follow the course of the river and get as far away from the coast as you can. There is plenty of opportunity in the towns of Manchester and Salford to find work and give yourselves a chance.'

'Where would we start?' asked Mary, 'and how far is it?'

'It is in the region of thirty miles to Manchester. I'll send word to Reuben in the morning,' said the priest. 'He'll put you on the right path, I'm sure of it.'

'Now before I find you some beds for the night,' he continued, 'I'd like to hear your confessions.'

He took them to the confessional in the chapel where in turn they poured out their tales.

Mary, though, through shame could not bring herself to mention Regan's abuse of her body.

The priest granted them absolution without penance, and afterwards led the young pair to a small room containing two narrow beds. The relief of having safe and secure accommodation for once was enough to send them both off quickly and soundly.

The following morning, they were given a breakfast of porridge, whilst the young serving girl went to summon

Reuben. While they were waiting, the priest Father Bene-dict asked 'Have you any money for your journey?'

'We have a little,' replied Mary.

'Well, I suggest you purchase some strong boots from the cobbler's shop just along the road,' said the priest. 'You have a long walk ahead of you.'

Smiling at Mary he added, 'By the way, your attempt to pass yourself off as a lad has not been very successful. I think you should also obtain hats and conceal your faces somewhat.'

Their saviour from the previous night arrived a short time later.

'Reuben,' said Father Benedict, 'will you escort our young friends to the riverside but keep well clear of the harbour. Show them the way towards Manchester, for I think their best hope is to leave our city of intrigue.'

'I'll do it gladly,' answered Reuben.

So, they took a fond farewell of the kindly priest, and started on the next stage of their journey to freedom.

Chapter Eleven

After purchasing some good leather boots and straw hats, they followed Reuben through the confusing warren of narrow shabby streets until they eventually found themselves at the riverside.

On the way, Reuben had regaled them with a little of his own life story. He'd been born on a sugar plantation in Barbados and been selected by his master James Penney to become his personal manservant. Penny had brought him to England and installed him in his mansion on the outskirts of the city.

Although his life was not unbearable, his desire for freedom was overwhelming, and he'd managed to run away in the dead of night. He'd headed for the dock area where there was a sizeable colony of freed black people and was quickly absorbed in their midst.

Eventually Penny had discovered his whereabouts and tried to drag him back to his life of enslavement. However, Penny hadn't reckoned on the power of a consortium of abolitionists who had successfully petitioned Parliament to pass an Act granting freedom to former slaves, and to his chagrin had to admit defeat.

Reuben was so grateful for his newfound freedom that he had vowed to give assistance to any fugitive, black or white, that he encountered and take them to Father Benedict.

He led Mary and Joe some way along the river, which was already beginning to become less broad.

'This is where I turn back,' he said. 'I don't know how far you'll have to travel. Just follow the river to wherever you feel safe to stop and Godspeed you on your way.'

The young couple and thanked him warmly. They shared a friendly embrace, and then it was off along the bank of the Mersey to wherever their destiny lay.

* * *

The digging of the ventilation shafts was continuing at great pace and by the Wednesday night of the following week, they had dug down to the required depth. A small army of bricklayers and their labourers were engaged on all the shafts and shoring the entrance to the tunnel.

Medlock's men in the meantime were one of several gangs employed in the wearisome task of puddling the existing dig.

Huge heaps of clay and heavy loam were brought along the Bridgewater, deposited on the banks of the new cut, and from there mixed with water and shovelled into the trench. Then it was spread over the bottom and sides of the trench, making a waterproof seal. There was no easy way to do this. It was a case of stamping it smooth with spade and boot, and repeating the process until the bottom layer was almost three feet thick. Exhausting heavy labour in the heat of early summer.

Saturday morning eventually arrived to the great relief of the entire workforce, and it being Whitsuntide, they were granted an extra day off.

Sam collected his wages and Mr Davies drew him to one side and said 'Now, Sam. Can ye ride a horse?'

'I have been up on a horse, before,' answered Sam, 'but I couldn't in truth say I was an expert.'

'No matter,' said Davies, 'my old mare Bessie is as good as gold. Ye can take her to go and visit your home. Ye said it's twenty mile or more. If ye leave now she'll get you there before dark.'

'Oh, thank you sir. That's a wonderful gift,' said Sam with delight.

'Just make sure ye return by Monday night,' said Davies.

'Oh, I will surely,' said Sam, and off he went along the Bridgewater, retracing his steps of a few weeks previously.

Bessie plodded sedately along the towpath, giving Sam no reason to test his scant riding skills. It was a changeable day, windy and showery and he was wet through by the time he approached his home. It had been a long day in the saddle and his thighs were aching intolerably. Nonetheless, nothing could dampen his joy at the prospect of being with his loved ones again.

It was almost dark by the time he arrived, but his mother Amy was still outside trying to shoo the last of the chickens into the safety of the coop. She heard the approaching horse and rider and ran into the cottage to warn her husband of a stranger's arrival, never thinking for a moment that it could be her returning son.

Sam called out from Bessie's back, 'Mother, Father, 'tis only me come home to see you all.'

He dismounted gingerly as Amy gasped in surprised delight. She rushed to Sam, covering his face with her kisses.

The reunion was a thing of great joy for the whole family. His mother clung to him, and his father shook his hand warmly. The younger children were roused from their slumbers and joined in the celebration, but of James there was no sign.

'Where's James?' asked Sam.

'Don't fret lad,' answered his father. 'Since you've been away, he's taken to walking out with young Rosie Corby over Flixton way. He'll be back directly - while there's still light to see.'

Sure enough, a few minutes later the young swain swung jauntily into view.

Sam was taken aback by the changes in his brother's appearance. The wispy beard had developed into a thing of some substance. Honey coloured and bushy, there was something of the Viking warrior about him. Sam was really quite envious.

The brothers embraced affectionately. Amy and Angela prepared food, and the whole family rejoiced in the return of their hero.

Sam presented his mother with four crown coins - most of his earnings over the past three weeks.

His father was fulsome in his praise of his second born.

'The good Lord bless you lad. It was a bold move that took you from us, but you kept your word and came back.'

'Ay, father,' replied Sam, 'I can stay only until Monday morn, and then I must return. I want ye to take the money. I have no need of it. We're well fed and housed at the dig.'

'Well, we'll not turn it down,' said Seth, 'I have in mind to buy a piglet from Jack King over the way. We can fatten it with scraps and let it root about in the spare field. A crown should do it.'

'That's great notion,' said Sam. 'Ye'll have meat for the winter, at last!'

The whole family plied Sam with questions about his experiences, long into the night, until eventually tiredness overwhelmed them, and they took to their various beds.

Whit Sunday dawned bright and clear, and the sun soon climbed and gave a perfect late spring day. The Burton family all attended church and the neighbours were all anxious to hear of Sam's exploits. He was quite the hero, and many a lad among his peers was keen to hear if there was an opportunity for them too.

Sam calmly dealt with all their questions, stressing how hard and dangerous the work could be.

One of their number, Robin Parkin, a boy of about Sam's age was particularly persistent and pleaded with Sam to take him along.

'I can't do that, Robin,' he explained. 'Ye'll have to do as I did and find your own way. Just follow the canal 'til ye come to the junction at Preston Brook.'

Monday came around all to quickly and it was time for a sad farewell.

'I don't know when I'll be back again,' he told his parents. 'We're getting further and further away, and I doubt they'll give me leave to come again for a while.'

'We'll get by son,' said his mother tearfully. 'Just come when ye can and don't forget us.'

'I'll never do that Ma,' vowed Sam. 'By hook or crook, I'll be back one day.'

'Take care, lad,' said his father, clasping Sam to his bosom.

Sam took his leave of his sorrowful kinfolk and set off on the day's ride back to Preston Brook.

Chapter Twelve

Mary and Joe walked all morning through the fresh green meadowland that bordered the river. For the first time since their flight had begun back in Wexford, they felt a sense of relief and freedom from anxiety.

They still had the gold watch and a little money left. They'd bought bread, cheese and apples from a barrow man before leaving the noisy sprawling city behind.

With the sun high above them, they sat down to consume some food in the shade of a huge oak tree. Their experiences had instilled a growing feeling of companionship and maturity that defied their youth.

'I reckon we'll be alright soon,' said Joe. 'We'll probably get to some big town and find work.'

'I hope you're right, Joe,' replied Mary. 'Maybe a big house, looking for a maid and a stable lad - that would suit us fine.'

'If they would take a pair of poor Irish riff-raff, like us,' she added, only half-jokingly.

They set off again across the countryside, keeping the river in sight on their right-hand. Flocks of sheep grazed the lush pastures in large fields enclosed by low stone walls. In other fields, crops of wheat and barley were already thriving, and there was a general air of prosperity that was a world away from their poverty-stricken homeland. From time to time, they passed some people working in the fields, but nobody seemed to be concerned about their passing by.

The strong daylight of late May slowly began to slip away, and the youngsters began to think about where they could spend the night undisturbed.

As dusk began to take hold, they came to an isolated farmhouse with several outbuildings. A couple of fierce sounding dogs gave notice of their approach, barking constantly. The door of the farmhouse opened, and a stout ruddy faced farmer with mutton chop whiskers hailed them.

'What the devil do ye want?' he shouted in a hostile tone.

'Please, sir,' answered Mary, 'we're travelling to Manchester and seek only a place to lay our heads for the night.'

'Be off with you. I'm sick and tired of ye thievin' Irish beggars,' cried the farmer.

He stepped out from his threshold brandishing a stout wooden staff.

'Get away now or I'll set dogs on ye.'

They had little choice but to comply and withdraw from that hostile situation.

By this time darkness had almost completely descended and they realised they had no choice but to rest in the lee of one of the stone boundary walls. They finished the last of their sparse provisions and huddling together tried to sleep.

In all their travels this was the only hostile response they'd had encountered since the confrontation with the gypsies on the road to Dublin. It was discouraging but they took heart from the thought that most people had helped them. There would always be those of a less tolerant bent, and such must be endured.

The following morning dawned unusually cool for the time of year and the two travellers started on their way stiff with cold and very hungry.

Nevertheless, they resolved to go on following the river until it led them to a better place.

As the sun climbed the day grew warmer and warmer. They trudged wearily along, passing several other farmsteads - never trusting their luck to find a welcome at one of them.

* * *

At length they flopped down, weak with hunger and exhaustion beside a rippling stream. They scooped copious amounts of the cool water with their hands.

'I can go no further Joe,' said Mary despairingly. 'We'll have to rest here for the night. Surely, we'll come to Manchester tomorrow.'

So, they hunkered down for the second night in the open countryside, wretchedly hungry and cold despite the mildness of the weather.

The next morning dawned bright and clear, and the sun quickly warmed their shivering bodies. They drank and washed from the brook and resumed their journey.

Before long, to their great relief, they could see on the horizon the spire of a church silhouetted against the cloudless sky.

The sight gave them heart and they made their way steadily towards it. As they drew closer and closer, they also began to see that what they were approaching was in fact a large town, built on a hill overlooking the river.

Soon they had reached the outskirts of the town. The riverside was vibrant with activity. Several ships and barges were moored and being loaded or unloaded with all manner of goods. The dwellings in the adjacent narrow lanes were a mix of humble thatched cottages and more prosperous two- and three-story stone-built houses and shops. As they warily made their way along one of the riverside lanes, they used some of their shrinking money supply to purchase some bread and smoked fish from a small store.

It was their first food for two whole days, and they dispatched it with relish.

They continued sauntering through the hustle and bustle of this thriving place, until they reached a junction with a wider road. The traffic here was even heavier - wagon loads of produce bound for the docks, mingled with dozens of pedestrians going about their business. It all seemed of great interest to the young couple and hinted at promising possibilities for them.

After a while, they came to a terrace of three-storied houses in various states of repair. Joe, who had a little understanding of the written word, discerned that a board outside one of the better ones stated that it was a lodging house.

They thought they must be far enough away from the coast to risk staying awhile, so Mary knocked on the stout wooden door of the house. The door was opened by a statuesque lady dressed in a long blue gown and shawl. Her black hair piled high gave her a somewhat haughty demeanour.

'Yes, my dears. What can I do for you?' she asked in an unmistakable Irish brogue, which seemed somehow at odds with her appearance. 'Is it lodging ye're seeking?'

'Yes, ma'am,' answered Mary. 'We've just arrived here in Manchester and will be seeking work as soon as we're settled.'

The woman laughed heartily.

'Lord, save us,' she chuckled, shaking her head. 'Ye're miles from Manchester, my dears. This is Warrington. You'd better come in, 'tis obvious ye're as green as the grass of our homeland.'

The interior of the house seemed singularly well kept and maintained. The landlady led them into a well-furnished parlour where despite the warmth of the season, a fire in the hearth gave a comforting glow to the room.

'Let me see about you,' said the lady. 'I'd say from your brogue ye're from the auld country, like myself, and you've crossed the ocean to seek a better life. Am I right?'

'That's correct, ma'am,' answered Joe.

'Well, I can offer ye lodging if ye can pay for it,' said the lady in a matter-of-fact way. 'Ye can share a room with two other such as yourselves at a half crown per week each. That'll get you a meal each day, as well.'

'That sounds fair,' said Mary. 'We'll be seeking work straight away. Is there much to be had?'

'Oh, aye surely,' answered the woman. 'A young lad will always get a day's work down at the docks, and as for ye, miss, well I'm sure something suitable will turn up.'

'Ye can start by dressing like the maid you are,' she added with a grin.

'It was easier for me to try to pass for a lad,' said Mary. 'I suppose it'll be alright now to be a girl again.'

'I'll find something for ye,' said the woman. 'Now I need your names and your first week's board.'

Mary been thinking for some time that a change of name and address for both of them would be another sensible step to cover their tracks. Before Joe could speak, she answered quickly and assertively. 'My name is Teresa Turley, and this is my brother Will. We come from Galway.' She had no idea where Galway was, it was just a name she'd heard somewhere in the past.

The woman wrote their names in a ledger on a writing desk. 'I think I'll call ye Teasy for short,' said the woman, 'and I'm Mrs Kelly from Dublin, but you can call me Kitty.'

'Well look Miss Teasy,' she went on, 'it wouldn't be seemly to put you in with three men, so you can share my room for a while.'

She continued in a severe tone, 'I run a respectable lodging house for my fellow countrymen, and at the first sign of trouble you'll be out on the street.'

'Oh no missus!' said Joe/Will. 'All we want is a chance of a new life of peace. There was precious little of it from whence we came.'

Kitty gave them a tour of the house. Leading off the parlour was a roomy kitchen with a black enamel cooking range and a row of pots and pans in a rack above. It reminded Teresa of the huge kitchen at Dunslaney – a memory that made her shiver momentarily. A large wooden table with six wooden chairs and a sturdy wooden dresser were the only other furniture. A door led to a cobbled yard and two primitive lean-to huts. One of them was the privy, and the other a wash house.

Upstairs there were four bedrooms, two of which were quite large, and up another flight of stairs two more much smaller rooms. All the rooms contained at least two beds, although the one Will would be sharing had three, with hardly any space to move between them.

To the young fugitives, it seemed they'd found a safe haven at last.

Chapter Thirteen

McClure and his men arrived dejectedly back at Dunslaney to face the fury and withering contempt of Fintan Regan.

'I'm very sorry, sir,' said the constable. 'We did all we could and came within a hairs breadth of catching them, but they must have boarded a ship for England.'

'A slip of a lass and a gossoon have made fools of ye all,' roared Regan, 'ah well so be it. See Delaney for your money, though ye've done precious little to earn it.'

As his rage gradually abated, Regan spent long hours in moody contemplation. The loss of the money and watch was a mere trifle but the theft of Prince, his pride and joy, gave him much sorrow. The animal had been quite simply the best he'd ever owned and, he had to admit, usually excellently turned out by young Joe Molloy. He had also to undergo the indignity of his inevitable loss of face among the local gentry.

The brooding resentment over being made a fool of slowly gave way to the realisation that, much to his confusion, the absence of Mary was the most overwhelming loss of all. It was grievously affecting his every waking moment.

He'd never previously given a whit for all the maids that had shared his bed, dismissing them all perfunctorily when he tired of them, yet somehow this girl Mary preyed upon his mind constantly.

The very fact that she'd had the courage and determination to run away was evidence of her spirit. It brought home to him his blindness in not recognising that this girl was different. Despite her lowly status, Fintan could imagine a life with Mary as the wife he'd done his best to avoid searching for.

The county set could go to blazes as far as he was concerned. Mary was the one for him and his mistreatment of her had driven her away.

He became more and more morose as the days lengthened and his restless nights were filled with remorse and shame thinking of the sweet lass who he'd wronged so badly. He'd callously used her to satisfy his own selfish urges. Such thoughts dominated his every waking moment.

His life thus far, had been one of idle luxury. His every whim was catered for by an army of servants, only too grateful for the escape from poverty that their employ provided.

He'd cared naught for the plight of the poor peasantry who provided him with the source of his wealth. He'd learned from a very early age to treat all and sundry with total indifference and to expect his word to be obeyed without question.

His father's lack of interest in him was manifested in a young man totally ignorant of the management of his estates and holdings, and he began to realise that the whole pattern of his life must change if he was ever to know peace of mind.

Furnished with this new zeal, he summoned Delaney, his accountants and legal advisors to a series of meetings in the library at Dunslaney, in order to receive comprehensive instruction into the day-to-day management of his affairs.

In spite of his decadent life to date he was not a dullard and quickly started to learn a little of just how his fortune had been amassed and various other aspects of the business. He took to visiting all parts of his domain on horseback and observing the hardship and extreme poverty of the very people whose toil provided his wealth.

His whole outlook on life began to undergo a profound change. He resolved to do everything in his power to improve the lot of his poor tenantry.

First of all, he decreed that none of his tenants would be evicted for non-payment of rent, and indeed they were to be helped to till their poor soil more efficiently. To this end he consulted a number of reputable agriculturists and arranged for huge amounts of manure and lime to be shipped in and distributed.

On his constant rounds, he took to giving advice on utilisation of the land to all and sundry.

He also discovered that after the tragedy of his mother's passing, his father had sought solace in the bottle, and bedding, like himself, a succession of his serving girls.

* * *

Despite his frequent bouts of drunken debauchery, Regan senior retained a good head for business and managed his affairs with resolution. The Dunslaney estate had prospered and grown under his stewardship.

One of his housemaids, a young slender lass of around twenty-five summers, had become his bed companion of choice. Her name was Elidh Molloy, the daughter of his head groom Diarmid.

Elidh was a practical girl who soon realised that subjecting herself to her master's will was her passport to a life of comparative comfort at the castle.

Her favoured status caused some disgruntlement among her fellow servants as she rose through the hierarchy. She quickly become answerable only to Joyce Brennan, the head housekeeper, and Hubert Jeffs, the butler. She bore her bedroom duties with resignation until almost inevitably she fell pregnant.

As was a commonly held belief of the time, her condition was deemed to be largely her own fault, and she received little sympathy from either the master or her fellow household staff.

Gerard Regan's only concession to her was that she was allowed to keep her post, and she had to be thankful for even that faint hint of mercy. Plenty of girls in a similar plight were shown the door.

The master's slight pang of conscience was enough to spare her from the gutter.

When her time came, the other women of the household forgot their collective resentment of her and rallied around to help her through the ordeal of her labour.

On a dark and dismal November morn in 1759, she was delivered of a healthy boy child.

After her confinement she was returned to the ranks as a humble maid, no longer welcome in the master's bed.

Gerard Regan showed as much interest in his illegitimate son as he did in his official heir, and so the infant Joseph was brought up by his grandparents, Diarmid and Sara, in a small cottage close by the stables.

Diarmid was the chief groom and undertook to teach the lad to follow in his footsteps. Elidh visited whenever she could. As the years passed the lad thrived in the loving care of the humble couple, and quickly became his grandfather's competent assistant. He had a natural ability and affinity with the horses in his care and learned to ride well at a very early age. He was always told that Elidh was his sister, and the old couple were his parents. Those of the household who knew the truth conveniently put the information to the back of their minds until it was all but forgotten.

* * *

The change in attitude and demeanour of the young master of Dunslaney was soon the talk of the county.

Many of his peers took to shaking their heads and wondering if Regan was losing control of his senses.

Their collective cynicism had no effect, and he threw himself into his newfound mission with a passion.

Gone was the drunken turpitude of his former life - replaced by a passion to learn all he could of good farming practices and land management.

The constant stream of young lasses brought to his bed chamber had also ceased, as he entered a phase of celibacy, longing despairingly only for the young girl who had wrought this change of heart.

He began to take Elidh into his confidence. Over the years she had regained some of her previous status, and when Joyce Brennan became too old to continue her duties, she was given a small pension, and Elidh became head housekeeper.

One night, when his longing for Mary had overwhelmed him, he sought solace from his wine cellar, and well into his cups he summoned Elidh to listen to his sorrowful meanderings.

'Elidh, dear friend,' he cried, 'if only I could turn back time, I'd be a very different man.'

'Hush now, master,' answered Elidh soothingly, 'it's never too late to change, and you're already doing noble things by the poor folk hereabouts.'

'You don't understand,' he continued, 'I'd give my right arm to have that dear sweet colleen back with me. I used her sorely and I would make her my wife if I could.'

He continued venomously, 'If only I could seize that brat Joseph who stole her and my horse, my God, I'd make him suffer!'

Elidh took a deep breath and prepared to share the secret she'd borne for long years. 'I have something of grave import to tell you sir, and the time has come to do it.'

Regan gave her an appraising look and said, 'Well get to it woman, if it's so important.'

Elidh struggled to utter the words, and after what seemed an age to Regan, she blurted out, 'The lad Joseph is not my brother – he's my son, and what's more your father was his father, too.'

'What nonsense is this woman?' bellowed Regan.

'Tis true sir, as God's my witness. After your mother died, he turned to me for solace. One thing led to another, and I fell pregnant.'

The silence was palpable as Regan digested this bombshell. After some moments and visibly shaken, he demanded. 'Who can substantiate your story? Surely someone else must know the truth of it?'

'The older servants such as Mr. Jeffs and old Mrs Brennan, know it's true.' Elidh's voice was barely above a whisper. 'My parents and of course your father knew it, but just as he ignored yourself, he wanted nothing to do with his other boy.'

'So, this wretch Joseph is of my blood, you're saying?'

'Joseph Molloy is your half-brother. That's God's truth.'

'Sweet Jesus,' muttered Regan. 'That's a hard thing to get my head around.'

'I had no good reason to tell ye before,' continued Elidh, 'but if you're so bent on trying to get them both to return, it's best for ye to know the true facts.'

Regan, visibly shaken by these revelations, said 'Leave me now, Elidh, give me time to take it all in. Good God, a brother I never knew I had!'

This devastating news had the effect of sobering Regan somewhat, and he sat for hours in his chair weighing up what he could do to right yet another wrong.

Although the injustice done to his younger half-brother was not of his making, his newly discovered charitable nature made him determined to put the matter right by whatever means he could muster.

Eventually he fell asleep where he was. He awoke in the early hours disorientated and shivering but resolved to find a plan to return the girl who'd stolen his heart and his newfound sibling to his bosom.

Chapter Fourteen

The fickle British summer was behaving in time-honoured fashion; some days where the rain poured down incessantly, interspersed with others of blazing heat.

This was all good news for the canal builders as it gave an abundant supply of water to fill the completed sections of the great project. A huge pair of wooden gates were installed a few hundred yards from the tunnel entrance to form a seal. The feeder streams were diverted via puddled channels to gradually fill the first section. In addition, the barrier between the new canal and the Bridgewater was carefully removed piece by piece until the two waterways were merged. Water for the Bridgewater was never a problem as it was constantly being pumped from the Worsley coal mines directly into the canal. The Duke was a major investor in the new canal, so had no objection to it being supplied from the original.

The workers continued the arduous and dangerous job of excavating the tunnel at Preston Brook.

At the bottom of the shaft, which was now completely brick-lined, rungs were set in to enable the workers to climb in and out, as a somewhat hazardous alternative to the bucket. They had begun to excavate horizontally. The digging was to be done in both directions, the aim being to meet the other gangs tunnelling towards them.

It was gruelling and strength sapping work in conditions of great humidity. Sam began to suffer somewhat from claustrophobia and was doing his best not to show his fear of working so far underground with just the light of a few candles to show the way. To add to their misery, the ground at the bottom of the shaft was full of water and their boots were soon filled with the muddy slime.

Medlock, realising that his men were rapidly becoming exhausted, decreed that work spells would be of thirty minutes instead of an hour. Despite this concession, there was a mutinous feeling among the whole work force at the dangerous and squalid conditions they were being expected to endure.

At the end of another hard slog of a day, as they trudged back to the camp the three Irishmen Matt, Tom and Gerard confronted Medlock with their grievances.

'Look now, boss, it's damnably hot and dangerous work ye're expecting us to do,' said Matt, their spokesman, 'and we reckon it's worth more than two shillin' a day.'

'Ay, I don't doubt it,' answered Medlock. 'But thy wages is nowt to do with me – I'll tek it up with Davies and see can we get ye a bit more.'

As good as his word Medlock sought a meeting with Davies.

'I reckon ye'll have trouble keeping these lads ont' job, Mr Davies,' he said. ''Tis devilish hot and hard work in t' tunnel.'

'What do you want from me George?' countered Davies. 'The job has to be done. They knew it weren't to be a bed of roses when they were took on.'

'Well I reckon another bob a day while they're underground would keep 'em quiet.'

'Three shillings a day?' said Davies. 'Have you taken leave of your senses man? Besides they'd only spend it on more drink.'

'The way I sees it,' replied Medlock. 'Ye've a good bunch of men here who don't mind graftin' for their dough, but ye have to treat 'em fair or they'll be away.'

'I dare say you're right George,' sighed Davies. 'I'll see what Bradshaw's got to say on the subject.'

Frederick Bradshaw was the Company secretary in charge of operational costs.

Medlock reported back to his men, and they were partly appeased by the fact he'd done what he could to raise their concerns.

Bradshaw visited the site to see for himself the conditions that the men were working in. It wasn't just Medlock's gang of course, for there were others working at the bottom of even deeper shafts along the whole three- quarter mile length.

An astute man, with a shrewd head for calculation, he quickly realised that if he was to avoid a full-scale mutiny or desertion by the workforce, money would have to be spent.

He had considerable authority over funding for the whole project and, after some careful deliberation, came up with what he hoped would be an acceptable solution.

He called all the foremen together and gave them his decision.

'The costs of this whole project are escalating alarmingly,' he began, 'but I can see that the men need a carrot dangled in front of them. I propose that every man working underground shall have an extra sixpence per day. When the tunnel is complete every man who stays the course, shall receive a bonus of three guineas.'

This proposition did indeed ease the disgruntled men somewhat and so they continued with their filthy and hazardous work.

May ended with a violent thunderstorm that held up the work for some days owing to the flooding of the tunnel both at the shaft bottom and the entrance. The only good that came from the downpour was that the finished section of the canal filled rapidly and was put to use immediately. Barges were brought from the Bridgewater filled with cargoes of bricks and pulled by horses as far as the mouth of the tunnel, in much larger quantities than was possible by horse and cart. The men were put to work loading and unloading these barges, enabling the bricklayers and masons to get on with lining the roof and walls.

During a lull in these proceedings, Medlock took his crew over the route of the tunnel to see the progress on the other side of the hill.

The other three ventilation shafts were in various stages of development and, as they descended the south side of the hill, they could see that considerable inroads had been made on the southern portal.

As far as the eye could see this mighty project was taking shape with a whole army of men digging the trench that would eventually extend for over ninety miles.

'As you can see men,' said Medlock. 'There's enough work to last ye all for years. When this 'uns done, there'll be plenty more. Men with experience like us will be worth their weight in gold.'

The hot sun of early June dried out the works sufficiently for work to resume in the tunnel. Sam had a brainwave that he put to Medlock.

'On the farm we used to dig holes to soak up the floodwater. If we dig a hole next to where we're working at the bottom, mebbe it'll drain away some of this accursed water.'

'By God, lad,' said Medlock, appraisingly, 'ye're full of clever notions. I can see thee going up in t' world!'

So they put Sam's idea to the test, and it worked well enough to dry the ground beneath their feet. Medlock was full of admiration for the competence and intelligence of his youngest worker and stored the information for future reference. In his estimation, Sam could soon become his right-hand man.

Chapter Fifteen

Teresa, as she was now to be known, quickly settled into life at Mrs Kelly's lodging house. They came to an arrangement where in exchange for her keep, she would assist the older woman in the running of the lodgings.

Will, in the meantime, soon found work at a livery stable down by the docks.

So, for the time being they felt reasonably secure and content, becoming more and more immersed in the alien environment of this bustling, prosperous town.

As the days turned into weeks, Teresa felt sufficiently at ease to take Kitty into her confidence and share some of her story with her.

Kitty listened open-mouthed as the young girl recounted the tale of their flight from Wexford.

'My God, girl!' she gasped. 'I thought my own tale worth telling 'til I heard yours.'

'So, you think there's still a band of men after you?' she continued, 'I reckon you'll be safe enough, there's scores of Irish people here who've fled the ould country, but I'll keep me ear to the ground for ye.'

Teresa's trust in this homely Dublin woman was growing stronger by the day. She began to accompany her on a daily round of shopping and calling in on friends and neighbours. Kitty adopted a policy of passing 'Miss Teasy' off as her niece, to deflect any curiosity. Teresa played her part well, assuming an air of humility and generally keeping a low profile.

She could tell that Warrington was a thriving town with plenty of work for all. She heard from Kitty that sail making for the Royal Navy and the merchant fleet was one of the main industries providing employment for hundreds.

There were also foundries producing copper and iron in vast quantities. All in all, it seemed that Will and herself could establish a new life here quite quickly.

Her feelings for her fellow fugitive were confusing to her. She had obviously become very fond of him, but in a sisterly fashion. Regan's abuse of her had left a feeling of total abhorrence towards the sex act, so although she cared very much for Will, it was in a purely platonic way.

Everything seemed to be going so smoothly, that it was almost inevitable that fate would one day deal a bitter blow.

* * *

Since the Mersey had been made navigable further inland some years previously, it was now possible for bigger ships to sail on the tide as far inland as Warrington. One such was the Foxhunter with a cargo of bales of linen for the sail makers.

One disastrous morning in mid-June, Will taking a break from his work at the stables, was strolling jauntily along the dockside.

Without a care in the world, he never thought to take note of the name of the ship that was being unladen at the wharf.

He was to pay dearly for his inattention. One of the deck hands recognised him as one of the stowaways from a previous trip and raised the alarm.

As Will continued his nonchalant stroll he became aware of the presence of running men behind him. In panic he started to run too but slipped on the greasy cobbles and went sprawling. He was hauled to his feet by a trio of tough sailors who tried to drag him, kicking and wriggling, back to the Foxhunter.

Some of the dock workers witnessed Will's desperate struggle to free himself. One of them, bolder than the rest shouted,

'Bloody press gang. They got my brother lately, damned if I let them get another young 'un.'

With that, the wharfman and two of his fellow workers began to tussle with the sailors, and a mighty fist fight broke out.

In the confusion of the melee, Will managed to free himself and for the second time in recent weeks, fled for his life through the mean alleys and lanes until he was far away from the river.

It had been a close shave and Will realised that their notion of having reached a safe refuge was just an illusion. Teresa and he would have to travel even further afield before they could even think of relaxing their guard.

In his headlong flight from the dockside, he'd wandered into a part of the town he'd never seen before, and it was well into the early evening before he got his bearings and managed to find the lodging house. Teresa greeted him at the door, her anxiety evident in her voice.

'Thank God ye're back,' she said. 'I was beginning to think ye'd been taken'.

'I damn near was,' replied Will.

He gave her the full details of his narrow escape. Teresa's face became fraught with fear and worry.

'Oh, Jesus,' she gasped, 'I thought all this was too good to be true. It's no good, we'll just have to move on.'

She had enough trust in Kitty to take her into her confidence and ask her advice.

'Well, ye'd better stay low here for a while,' said Kitty. 'I'll soon find out if they're still hunting ye. Keep away from the stables lad. I know Tom Warland the owner. I'll tell him ye're in a bad way with a fever and get any money he owes ye.'

The following morning Kitty sought information from various of her contacts. She learned that the officers and crew of the Foxhunter had soon given up the hunt for young Will in the face of the surge of opposition from the wharf-siders. The ship had sailed on the evening tide, and the excitement of the morning had soon been forgotten.

Despite Kitty's confident opinion that they'd be as secure here as anywhere, the nagging doubt and fear of capture weighed heavily on the minds of the young couple.

'I just don't feel safe enough here, Will' said Teresa anxiously.

'But where can we go to that would be?' replied Will, 'seems like they're set on taking us back to face the scaffold.'

'We mustn't give up' said Teresa firmly, 'let's try our luck in Manchester. Mrs. Kelly says it's much bigger, and we'd have a chance to lose ourselves there.'

Next day they discussed their options with Kitty.

'Ay, surely,' said the older woman, 'Manchester's twice the size of this place, and there's plenty of work. These new-fangled cotton mills are springing up all over, so they say. Ye'd have a better chance of melting into the background there, so to speak.'

She went on, 'Tis a grim place though so I'm told. Smoke belching out from the factories all day and night. Hot and noisy.'

The youngsters thought it over and announced that they were going to try it.

'Well, I think you could walk there easy enough in two days,' said Kitty, 'just follow the river like you did to get here. There'll be plenty like yourselves there, it's full of Irish folk I'm told.'

So, Teresa and Will began to make their preparations for yet another flight.

Before they left, Kitty called them into her parlour and made a chance remark that was to alter the course of their lives profoundly.

'I'll be sorry to lose ye both, especially you Miss Teasy,' she said, 'but, afore ye go, I've thought of another thing you might try. I've heard of a mighty project that's going on, not too far away.'

'Oh, what is it?' asked Teresa.

'Warland told me that there's a big canal being made to link the Duke's cut with big towns to the south.'

'What's the Duke's cut?' asked Will.

'It's the canal they made a few years ago to carry coal to Manchester, and it's only a wee bit from here. I'd say there'd be work for both of ye, and nobody to come chasing after ye.'

'How do we get there?' asked Teresa.

'Just follow the river back the way ye came until you reach a big house called Norton Priory. I think ye'd be almost there. Ye're looking for a spot called Preston Brook, so Warland told me.'

'What do ye think, Will?' asked Teresa.

'Might as well, Manchester don't sound very wholesome,' replied Will, little knowing what a tragic option he'd chosen.

Chapter Sixteen

At Dunslaney castle, a fortnight or so later, news filtered through to Regan that Joseph had almost been arrested in the town of Warrington, confirming that the fugitives had travelled over the sea as he had feared.

So strong was his yearning to return the wronged couple to his bosom, that Regan made the momentous decision that he must take matters into his own hands.

He sent for the ever efficient and reliable Delaney to discuss his plans.

'Francis,' he began, 'I shall have no peace until I have resolved certain matters. To do that I must go across the sea and endeavour to find the fugitives myself. I trust in you to manage my affairs until I return, and to keep up the practices of management that I have put in place.'

'That will be done sir, assuredly,' replied Delaney. 'Have ye any notion how long ye'll be away?'

'As long as it takes,' said Regan. 'I'll search the length and breadth of England if I have to.'

'It would be advisable, sir,' continued Delaney, 'to not undertake this mission alone. I think I can find you a pair of trustworthy travelling companions in the town.'

'Ay, that would be sensible I suppose,' mused Regan. 'If ye're sure you can find such a pair but make haste man. The trail grows colder by the day.'

Regan then called Elidh to discuss his plans.

'I swear I shall bring them back home, good woman, and return your boy to you, or die in the attempt.'

He continued, 'I've a mind to take young Henry with me for he seems a bright young lad and he can serve as my man.'

Elidh swallowed hard and prepared to impart yet another momentous revelation to her master.

'Do ye not realise, sir, just who young Henry is?' Elidh spoke in an anxious tone.

'Don't tell me there's yet another brother?' retorted Regan. 'Lord above is that possible?'

'No sir, he's not your brother, he's your son.'

There was a moment of dumbfounded silence and then perplexed, Regan gasped. 'What, this surely cannot be true?'

'His mother was young Ellen Geraghty,' continued Elidh.

'Oh, God yes,' said Regan, wistfully. 'I remember her, sure I was no but a lad myself. What happened to her?'

'She was taken in by the priest Father Philip,' answered Elidh, 'but the child was raised here at the castle, because it was known that he was of your own blood. What happened to the mother after that, I couldn't say.'

'Oh, Mrs Molloy,' cried an aghast Regan. 'What dreadful sins have been committed here by my family. How can they ever be righted?'

'Tis the way of the world, sir,' said Elidh. 'Just how things have always been.'

'Bring the boy to me, please,' entreated Regan. 'Does he know aught of this?'

'No sir,' answered Elidh. 'He knows nothing of his parentage. Please take care when you tell him.'

When Henry was summoned to his master's presence, he approached with trepidation, wondering what he had done wrong.

He knocked timidly at the door to the master's drawing room.

'Come in, Henry lad,' boomed Regan. 'Stand in front of me 'til I get a good look at ye.'

Noticing the boy's anxious countenance, he said gently, 'Don't be nervous, Henry. I have something to tell you that ye're going to find hard to believe. Sure, I've only learned of it myself in the last hour. Now I can see in the light we surely have a likeness, lad. Come here.'

Henry approached with great concern, mystified as to what the master had in mind. He was shocked when Regan grasped him in a fierce embrace.

'I'm your father my boy.' He choked on the words. 'My God son, I have an overwhelming duty to put things right between us.'

Totally bewildered by this information, Henry stood shaking like a leaf.

Regan sat down on the chaise longue and spoke, 'Come sit with me awhile, until we find the right words to say.'

Henry, at fourteen, was already filling out and growing tall, with dark curly hair and the same blue eyes as his father. In fact, sitting next to one another the resemblance was striking, leaving no doubt as to the truthfulness of Elidh's revelation.

Regan summoned Elidh and asked her to assemble the whole workforce in the hall.

Some of the more senior among them had always known of Henry's lineage, but to most of them it came as a huge surprise. The under butler, Reginald Fox, had more to fear than most as he'd always bullied Henry unmercifully. He began to fear for his future.

Poor Henry, still in total shock and disarray, stood beside Regan as he imparted his joyous news to the household.

'Come my boy, your boot cleaning days are over. Mrs Molloy, please prepare a chamber for my son. I know you've all had a shock today, but I wager not nearly as big as my own. Master Henry is forthwith to be treated with all the respect that his new rank demands.'

* * *

In Warrington, Teresa and Will were making their preparations for the next stage of their quest for a new life, beyond the ever-present threat of the gallows. Some days previously, Teresa had shown Regan's watch to Kitty and asked her how much she thought she could sell it for.

'I have no notion of its real worth,' said Kitty, 'but if ye're caught with it, ye'll go a' swinging I'd say. I'll give ye four guineas, which'll be a big help to ye.'

Teresa readily accepted the older lady's offer, mightily relieved to be rid of the burden that she'd regretted snatching almost from the moment her impulsiveness had made her do it.

With Will's earnings from the stables and after settling with Kitty, they found they had a total of almost eight pounds with which to begin their flight. Kitty had found them both a change of clothing and trimmed the girl's hair again to maintain the flimsy disguise.

It was with a tearful farewell that they parted from their homely no-nonsense hostess.

They managed to find a narrow lane that led down to the riverside somewhat downstream from the dock area. They walked all morning and well into the afternoon. Eventually they got a glimpse of the red brick walls of the grand house, Norton Priory, that had been built adjacent to the ruins of the old medieval monastery.

They approached the house cautiously, mindful of the mixed response from previous encounters. It was their intention just to seek further directions, but actually they were to be spared from that dilemma.

They had crested a rise and could see below them, at some distance, horse drawn barges slowly gliding along a waterway.

It was, in fact, almost a replica of the sight that had greeted the Burton brothers all those weeks previously - the bustling traffic of the Bridgewater canal.

With renewed vigour they descended the hillside and began to walk along the towpath and very soon caught up with one of the coal-laden barges.

'Excuse me sir,' asked Mary of the boatman leading the horse, 'are we going the right way toward Preston Brook?'

'No, 'tis a couple of miles in the other direction,' replied the man. 'If ye put an inch to your step, ye'll make it before nightfall.'

And so, sure enough, the youngsters reached the junction of the two canals an hour or so later, just as the workforce was returning to base at the end of another arduous day's toil.

With some trepidation the young couple approached the complex of buildings. Davies just happened to be standing in the doorway of his office. He spotted Will and Teresa hovering nervously at the entrance and beckoned them over.

'Can I be of assistance to you?' he asked.

'My brother and I were told they may be work here,' answered Teresa apprehensively.

'Ye both seem very young to be seeking employment, I don't think there'd be anything suitable for you here. Are ye Irish?'

'Yes sir,' said Will defiantly. 'We're from Galway, where there's nothing for us except to starve to death.'

'That's as maybe, my lad, but nothing to do with me,' answered Davies shortly. 'Besides, it's strong handy men we're seeking, not youths of such slight stature as yourselves.'

'I've worked with horses all my life,' responded Will. 'Is there not a chance of stable work I could do?'

'Let me think on it overnight,' answered Davies. 'Ye can have food and a bed for the night, we'll not turn ye away hungry.'

He led them to the communal area where they were fed and allocated a palliasse each in a small empty tent. After their long walk and generous helpings of food they soon slept soundly despite the noises from the rest of the camp.

On the following morning, Davies called them into his office.

He addressed Will, 'You say ye have knowledge of horses, boy. Can ye shoe a horse?'

'No sir,' answered Will. 'But I'm willing to learn.'

Davies looked him up and down and at length, and said, 'So be it. Our blacksmith is seeking an apprentice, and I'm prepared to give ye a start, at six shillings a week, less two for your keep.'

Turning to Teresa he went on, 'As for you miss, you too are fortunate. There is work here with the other women, cleaning and cooking, if ye want it. There will be no payment but a roof over your head and good food.'

'Thank you, sir,' they said in unison. 'We won't let you down.'

It seemed to the young fugitives that at last they'd found a place where their desperate flight might end.

Chapter Seventeen

The work on the Trent and Mersey or Grand Junction as it was also known continued all summer. The weather had settled down into a fine warm July and considerable progress was made on all fronts.

Will and Teresa quickly settled into the routine. The young lad threw himself enthusiastically into his role as the blacksmith's apprentice and in no time at all became adept at making horseshoes, tools and other metal work. Teresa was taken under the wing of the other Irish ladies, helping with the cooking and cleaning. Playing their role of siblings meant they were allocated a tent of their own and felt at last some semblance of a peaceful existence after the trauma of their flight from Ireland and the threat still hanging over them.

Medlock's gang were still toiling away underground, where progress was slow and arduous. Inch by perilous inch the gangs were getting closer to the point where they would meet. Frequent rockfalls delayed them - an unnerving experience to be endured with as much stoicism as they could muster.

Sam, at Medlock's suggestion, was given time to gain some experience of the bricklayer's trade, and also some elementary joinery. George had recognised that this young man would make an ideal assistant to him, and the more useful skills that he could absorb, the better for his progression.

More labourers came to replace some of the injured and the disillusioned who found the work too dangerous, including a red headed Irishman, Tom Reilly. Of medium build, which belied his great strength, Reilly was a surly, ill-tempered type, who kept himself very much to himself. At the end of each day, he made no attempt to join the general joviality of his workmates. To a man they were all very wary of him. Any attempt at friendliness was rebuffed by the sullen newcomer, and they soon learned to leave him be.

* * *

At Dunslaney, young Henry was coming to terms with his new life.

His father, intent on making up for his wrongdoings of the past, bestowed much care and affection on the boy, leaving him in an air of bewilderment. His world had been completely turned on its head.

Servants, used to boxing his ears and ordering him about, now showed him due deference. Fox in particular kept well out of his way, although Henry had shown no animosity towards him. The complete changes of the circumstances had him pinching himself in disbelief

Every morning was taken up by an intensive course in equestrianism. A tutor was employed to improve his reading and writing.

At the same time his father was proceeding with feverish haste on his planned voyage to England to search for his beloved girl and wronged half-brother.

Delaney had procured two of the men, Mahoney and Fagan, who'd been part of the original search party as an armed escort, to ride as far as Dublin. There they were to be dismissed whilst Regan and his son would sail to Liverpool to take up the search in earnest.

There were, however, to be several weighty legal and commercial matters that could not be settled immediately, including the obtaining of letters of credit to a prominent Liverpool bank to finance the journey.

So, much to Regan's frustration, the summer was almost over, and it wasn't until early September that everything was set in place. The small band of travellers set off for Dublin. Henry rode with his father in the coach with the two horsemen on either side.

Three days later, after a rapid and incident free journey, they set sail on the evening tide, for Liverpool aboard the Greyhound, sister ship of the Foxhunter.

On the voyage Regan tried to explain to Henry the reasons for the mission, hoping to strengthen the bond between them.

Henry was still disconcerted and uncomfortable with his new role in life and found it difficult to return the affectionate attention that was being so lavishly poured on him.

He was astonished to learn that Joe, the stable lad, was actually his uncle, and that Mary, the humble chamber maid, was the object of his father's passionate quest.

However, showing a shrewd wisdom far beyond his years, he kept his own counsel, and tried to play his new role as a cherished son to the best of his ability.

* * *

The weather grew unsettled and made for a stormy crossing that blew the ship off course on occasion. The journey lasted for eight frustrating days in which both Regan and Henry suffered debilitating bouts of sea sickness. Confined to their cabin as the ship pitched and rolled in the mountainous waves, they became more and more wretched and weak from lack of sustenance. The storms eventually abated, and the captain was able to get Greyhound back on her course. Eventually they were relieved of their misery and disembarked at the dockside in Liverpool.

A carriage took them to the Royal George, an imposing hotel on the waterfront. Recently converted from an ordinary tavern to cater to the ever-growing number of well to do travellers, the Royal George was the last word in sumptuous luxury to rival the best that London had to offer.

Once again Henry was perplexed by the opulence of his surroundings and wondered when the bubble was going to burst as it surely must.

Despite the comfortable amenities offered by this fine place, impatience drove Regan to hire a carriage to continue their journey to Warrington. The next ship wasn't due for some days and time was of the essence as far as Regan was concerned, especially given the delay afforded by the protracted voyage from Dublin.

It became quite a hazardous journey. The road was poor and rutted, tossing them around mercilessly inside the carriage. Some two hours after leaving the hotel, they heard an exchange of angry curses and shouts, and the carriage came to an abrupt halt. A gang of four or five footpads had accosted them and commanded them to climb out.

Regan, however, had been half expecting such an occurrence, and ordering Henry to crouch down, he drew a pair of small pistols from a box he'd placed on the floor. With great care he primed and loaded them.

Suddenly, the carriage door was flung open and two leering faces appeared.

'Good day, to you gentlemen,' said one of them leeringly, displaying a set of rotting teeth. 'Please be good enough to step outside.'

Coolly Regan discharged both the pistols at them. The man with the blackened teeth took the full shot straight in his face and was killed instantly. The rest of them scattered hastily to the four winds. As the gun smoke cleared, Henry, visibly shaken by the encounter and Regan's cool response, looked on in newfound admiration for the steely resolve of his hero father.

'Be prepared for any eventuality,' said Regan. 'A valuable lesson for you Henry.'

The body of the dead robber was dumped unceremoniously by the roadside. Earnest discussion then took place between Regan, the driver and guard regarding the outcome of the incident. It was agreed that as nothing could be done for the dead man, it would be better for all concerned to forget it ever happened – his fellow miscreants were hardly going to report it, and so they resumed their bone-shaking journey.

They finally arrived in Warrington in the early evening and found comfortable lodging at The Red Lion Inn on Bridge Street, the main thoroughfare of the town.

Although not as lavish as their previous hostelry, The Red Lion proved to be a pleasant hostelry serving good food.

Regan was well satisfied and pleased that he'd found a decent base from which to organise his search. On the very next morning he began to make preliminary enquiries, enlisting the help of the desk clerk.

Chapter Eighteen

Will had quickly settled into his new job and was proving to be an able apprentice. The blacksmith, Sydney Cox, was well pleased with his progress.

Then one morning fate landed a devastating blow. New, untried horses were constantly being brought to the stabling area. As the work progressed, more and more bricks, timber and other materials were in constant transit. Fresh horses were an essential ingredient in the supply chain.

A young skittish grey colt was brought into the forge to be shod. Will could tell that the animal was extremely nervous and using all his experience spent some minutes trying to soothe him enough to receive his new shoes.

When he thought the horse was sufficiently calm, he led him into the smithy. He fixed the shoe to the left hind leg quickly and efficiently, but a sudden shower of sparks from inside the forge unnerved the colt and he kicked out his back legs and caught Will full in the face. He fell backwards and cracked his skull against an anvil as the colt bolted from the scene.

Will had been knocked unconscious and blood was streaming down his face from a deep gash in his temple. Davies was summoned and he, Cox and a couple of other labourers carried the stricken lad on a litter to the tent that had been set aside as a rudimentary first aid shelter.

Teresa and the other Irish women were quickly in attendance and bathed and dressed poor Will's terrible wounds, but the lad showed no sign of regaining consciousness. The surgeon, Mr Ralph Towers from the village, attended late in the afternoon but could do little more than apply a salve made from willow bark to relieve the pain.

'There's nothing else I can do for the lad,' he said shaking his head. 'All you can do is watch and pray to the Lord above to save him.'

Teresa was beside herself with anxiety. They'd been through so much together in the previous weeks, surely it couldn't end like this. All day she sat beside the stricken lad, sobbing with grief.

The other women shared Teresa's vigil. They took turns at sitting by his side, praying for him, talking soothingly to him, willing him back from his coma - all to no avail. After three days and never once regaining consciousness, the poor gallant youth succumbed to the terrible injury and died in Teresa's arms. The tragic irony, of course, was that neither he nor Teresa knew that back in Wexford he was part heir to a fortune.

A hasty funeral, paid for by the Company, was arranged at nearby Preston on the Hill, and poor Will's body placed in a plain coffin and buried in the graveyard.

A heavy pall of shock and misery descended on the whole site. Although Will and Teresa were newcomers, they'd quickly been accepted by the entire work force.

Teresa, in particular, with her happy, cheerful manner was a favourite with the other women who treated her as a young sister.

These good women did what they could to console the wretched girl, but her grief was all consuming.

Although Will and she had never had more than a chaste and honest relationship, their adventures together had forged a close loving bond and her despair was overwhelming.

She withdrew into herself, going through the motions of her daily tasks and spending long hours just staring into space. She wondered what she'd done to deserve the tragedies of losing everyone she'd ever held dear and wondered if there would ever to be an end to her misery.

She took to wandering aimlessly in the woods and fields of the neighbourhood, and her behaviour came to the notice of Tom Reilly.

* * *

Reilly, an Ulsterman from Tyrone, embittered by his harsh upbringing, had been treading a lone path for many years. His childhood had been spent in one of the less impoverished parts of Ireland. His father Hugh was the agent for a large estate near Omagh, owned by an absent English milord. Hugh was an ill-tempered, violent bully whose wife, two sons and a daughter lived a life in constant fear of his fists or boots. Tom had been beaten savagely for the slightest misdemeanour, and vowed he'd get away as soon as he was old enough.

At the age of seventeen, he decided he'd had enough.

His father had started on him once too often and one night, dodging under a wild punch to his head, Tom hit his father hard in the midriff, knocking him to the ground.

As the winded bully lay supine, gasping for breath, Tom kicked him in the groin, and without a word of farewell to his mother or siblings, grabbed his coat and ran like the devil, never to return.

He made his way vaguely eastward, begging, stealing and occasionally working on farms until he reached Belfast.

He signed on as a deckhand on a schooner and as soon as the ship docked at Liverpool, he drew his pay and left.

As the years passed, he continued to live on his wits, finding work on farms and the cotton mills that were springing up throughout the north.

He never stayed in one place for long. Fights with factory foremen and fellow workers kept him on the move.

These sociopath tendencies include a lecherous bent – he believed all women to be fair game to be preyed upon, as many an irate husband or father could testify.

One of his few attributes was a willingness to toil hard. at any job he was given. He'd never had any trouble finding work, and he took to "navvying" on the canal with some relish.

* * *

On one warm August evening Teresa was drifting in her usual state of confusion through the woods and stopped to rest on a fallen tree stump in a cool glade. Reilly, who had become adept at stealthily pursuing her for more than a week, suddenly jumped out of the bushes, startling her greatly.

A pretty lass like you shouldn't be out here all alone,' he said, 'come now, make room for me to sit beside you.' 'Go away, leave me alone,' pleaded Teresa.

'Ah now, just one little kiss for a lonely man.'

He put his arm around her and tried to force his mouth onto hers. She managed to wriggle free and began to run back to the site, but in her haste, she tripped on a tree root and fell.

Quick as a flash, Reilly jumped on top of her, pinning her down and began to tear at her clothing. She screamed for help at the top of her voice.

'Hold that noise, girl,' he barked hoarsely. 'There's nobody here but us and I'm going to take what I want so you might as well stop your struggling.'

He couldn't have been more wrong.

Sam Burton was also out and about setting his snares as usual. He heard the girl's desperate cries for help and came running on to the scene. He launched a powerful kick at Reilly's back and then using all his considerable strength hauled the abuser to his feet.

Reilly recovered quickly from the surprise attack and threw a mighty punch at Sam, which caught him on the side of the head and sent him staggering.

'Run for your life, miss,' Sam managed to gasp to Teresa.

She needed no second bidding and fled the scene sobbing in terror.

Although Sam had never been involved in a fight before, his sense of outrage at Reilly's assault of the hapless girl gave him guile and strength that he never knew he possessed. As Reilly closed on him, Sam managed to evade the next wild punch and delivered a telling one of his own to Reilly's ribs. The Irishman gasped for breath. Sam punched him hard on the jaw and he went down like a felled tree.

Sam stood over him and said, 'Keep your filthy hands to yourself in future, Tom, or there'll be more of the same for ye.'

With that he made his way back to the camp, rubbing his sore knuckles.

Teresa had blundered through the trees and made it back to the campsite where Liz Mulryan and Annie Docherty embraced her and tried to calm her.

A few minutes later, Sam appeared on the scene and anxiously enquired after Teresa. The Irishwomen, assuming that he was the cause of the young girl's distress, immediately began to berate him.

'Be off with you, you dirty whoreson,' shouted Liz shrilly. 'How could you treat her so, when you know what she's going through?'

Poor Sam, rendered speechless by these false assumptions, stood awkwardly in front of the screaming scolds, until the young victim came to his rescue.

'Oh, no,' she beseeched the women. 'Ye have it wrong. This boy was the one that saved me. It was that new one, Reilly who attacked me.'

Liz and Annie grudgingly conceded their mistake, still eyeing Sam with some suspicion, not totally convinced of his innocence.

Teresa elaborated further on the full details of her ordeal, but by this time, Sam had discreetly retired from the scene and returned to the men's quarters.

* * *

Like most of the young men of the workforce, Sam was in awe of the beautiful young Irish girl with such a tragic background. However, he had scant knowledge of the art of wooing, and resolved himself to admiring her from a distance.

He appointed himself as her bodyguard and kept a watchful eye on the brooding Reilly. Word had quickly spread throughout the camp and Reilly was completely ostracised by most. His foreman, Simms, was loathe to dismiss him, however, for despite his antisocial behaviour, he was a good reliable worker and there were too few of those around.

Reilly was part of gang working at the south portal, so their paths never crossed during the working day. Nonetheless Sam kept his wits about him at all times. His instinct told him that Reilly would not let it rest.

* * *

A few nights after Reilly's assault, Teresa once again strayed into the woods, and Sam made it his business to follow her at a respectful distance, checking his traps and setting new ones as he did so.

Teresa's meandering route took her to the same tree stump where Reilly had mounted his assault, and she sat down to get her breath.

Sam, keeping a watchful eye on her from behind a huge oak tree, accidentally trod on a twig. The resulting crack shattered the silence and Teresa rose with a shriek and looked around her in panic.

Sam emerged from his hiding place and approached her.

'Don't be alarmed miss,' he said softly. ''Tis only me. I mean ye no harm.'

'Oh, thank God,' gasped Teresa. She ran toward him in relief. It seemed the most natural thing in the world for Sam to enfold her in his arms, and they stood for some moments in a warm silent embrace.

At length Teresa said, 'I've been trying to find a way to thank you for saving me on that night but didn't know how to do it.'

'Think naught of it,' answered Sam. 'Any decent minded man would have done the same.'

He continued 'If ye'll pardon me, miss, I really don't think you should wander off alone of an evening. I'd be glad to accompany ye if ye don't think me too forward to say so.'

'Of, course I don't mind, Sam,' she answered. 'Is it all right if I call you Sam?'

'If you let me call you Teresa,' replied Sam, blushing in confusion.

So, they slowly made their way back to the campsite. She slipped her hand into his strong, calloused one, and felt a tingle of excitement coursing through her veins.

They'd almost cleared the trees when Sam dropped the brace of rabbits that he'd been carrying and pulled her to him.

'Can I kiss you, Tess? he murmured. 'Or is that a step too far?'

She answered by turning her face up to his and they shared their first embrace.

To Teresa that first kiss was such a complete contrast to the ones she'd been forced to endure from Fintan Regan. A soft trembly kiss that grew in intensity as it continued.

For Sam, it was the first time in his life that he'd kissed a girl, and he knew there and then that he'd never want to kiss another. They broke off just long enough to whisper endearments to one another, and then kissed again and again.

When, at last their loving embrace came to an end, they made their way into the settlement keeping a chaste distance, lest tongues started to wag.

It was already too late, however. The knowing ladies of the camp had already scented a waft of romance in the air and greeted the bashful couple with hearty whoops of delight.

* * *

As the summer progressed their love blossomed and grew stronger by the day. For Teresa it was as if a miracle had happened. She had thought that the despair and trauma of her losses - first her whole family in the winter and spring, and then the faithful young Will - was such a grievous loss that she'd never recover.

Such are the healing properties of headlong, breathless love that she had a completely new outlook on life and looked forward to every new day with a vigour and joyousness she'd never thought possible.

For Sam, used only to the humdrum life on his parents' farm, falling in love with this beautiful young innocent lass was the best thing that had ever happened to him. The long hours spent in the claustrophobic surrounds of the tunnel seemed to fly by, and he was teased unmercifully by his workmates.

Every night they could be seen strolling hand in hand through the surrounding countryside, stopping every few moments to indulge in their mutual ardour. Such was their joy in each other that they were oblivious to the glowering Reilly who had taken to stalking them from a distance, looking for an opportunity for revenge against Sam and perhaps another attempt to have his way with the young maid.

Chapter Nineteen

By mid-August, work in the tunnel was sufficiently advanced for the various work parties to be able to faintly hear one another's endeavours as they approached the point of convergence. The extra wages and the promise of the large bonus were enough to spur them on, despite the dreadful hazards.

One morning as Sam, Matt and Tom were hacking away at the face as usual, they heard a rumbling sound behind them, and suddenly a large section of the roof gave way. They were engulfed in a shower of earth and stone. Although thankfully not injured, they were trapped by the huge pile of debris that had been dislodged. The candles had all been obliterated and they were left in pitch blackness to add to the trauma of the calamitous situation. They began to pick frantically at the mound.

Sam, it seemed, was keeping a much cooler head than his companions and took charge of the situation.

'Come boys,' he said calmly. 'Let's just sit tight and wait for the others to dig us out. There's not much air down here, so we need to save as much as we can.'

Medlock quickly organised a rescue party, and although they worked quickly and methodically, it was almost three hours before they reached their stricken comrades.

Medlock, realising that it would be nigh impossible to persuade them to descend into the pit again that day, told them to take the rest of the day off. They trudged back along the towpath to a welcome bath and change of clothing, quaffing copious amounts of ale to blot out the nightmarish memory of their ordeal. That night Medlock gathered his men together and tried to rally and cajole them into returning to the hell hole of the tunnel. An atmosphere of mutiny, however, was prevalent among the entire work force, and there was a very real threat of the entire operation grinding to a halt.

Bradshaw, Davies and some other worthies of the company realised that they had a crisis on their hands. It seemed that increased financial inducements were not going to be enough to persuade the men back to the dig, but a compromise solution was at hand.

Several of the local farmers had petitioned the canal company to release some of the work force to help bring in the harvest.

Pragmatism won the day and the Company officials realised that giving the men a break from the navigation might be enough to dissuade them from quitting in their droves. So, on the following morning Davies announced to the assembled work force that any man who wished to avail himself of the four shillings a day that was being offered by the farmers in the area, was free to leave the dig for the three weeks or so until the harvest was gathered in.

The majority of the work force seized the opportunity eagerly, and so for a month, encompassing the latter half of August and early September, work on the great enterprise came to a virtual standstill as most of the navvies set off for the various local farms.

Sam had a major dilemma to wrestle with. On one hand he felt duty bound to return to the family farm to help with the harvest. However, he was so wrapped up in his newfound love, he was reluctant to part from her even for a few weeks.

Teresa and he discussed the matter earnestly as they strolled out together on one of their regular evening trysts.

'I hate to leave you, my darling girl,' said Sam wistfully. 'But I fear I may have to go. My parents will be expecting me to return and pitch in.'

'Sam,' she replied. 'Of course, you must go. You'd never forgive yourself if you let them down. I'll be fine staying here with the other women.'

'I'm fearful that evil, good for nothing Reilly might try to molest you again,' said Sam, anxiously, 'I don't think that he'll be leaving to work on a farm.'

'I'll be very careful. I promise not to leave the camp on my own. Just come back to me as soon as you can. I'll miss you every day you're away.'

They clung close to each other, safe and secure in their love.

The next day, courtesy of Davies lending him Bessie again, Sam set off back to his home. Before he left, he had a long talk with George Medlock, who had no plans to leave the camp, preferring to stay and keep an eye the few workers who'd decided that farm work was not for them.

'George,' said Sam, who was now on first name terms with his gaffer, 'I'll be worried sick that Reilly will try something with my lass. Can I beseech you to keep her safe for me.'

'Ay, of course I will,' replied Medlock. 'Don't fret on that score, lad. Just get thysen back as soon as ye're able.'

So, after a tearful farewell embrace with his beloved Teresa, Sam mounted the trusty old mare and set off on the twenty or so miles back to his home.

After a long day in the saddle, he arrived back at the farmstead in the early evening to the usual joyous reception.

He proudly handed over a sum of five pounds to his mother.

'Oh, my lovely boy' she gasped. 'Never have we had such riches, I'm so proud of you.'

Over the course of the next two weeks, the whole country was blessed with some fine late summer weather and the bumper harvest was brought in safely, much to the relief of Seth.

A huge harvest supper involving several of the neighbouring farmsteads was laid on and the humble countryfolk feasted and danced well into the night. James had brought the comely Miss Rosie Corby and announced to all and sundry that he'd asked for her hand and been accepted. This was the cue for Sam to tell of his own newfound love. He'd expected the same back slapping congratulations afforded to his brother, but when he'd mentioned that Teresa was Irish there was a distinct wariness in the atmosphere.

His father in particular wasted no time in making his feelings known.

'You be very careful there my lad,' he said shaking his head. 'The Irish are nobbut gypsies and beggars. I never met a good one yet.'

'No father,' said Sam, defiantly, 'she's a wonderful, sweet natured lass who's been through hell to get here, and I'm very fond of her.'

'Well, you're old enough to know your own mind by now,' said Seth. 'But I doubt it'll last. You need one of our own, like your brother has found. Apart from that, the Irish are all damned Catholics.'

His father's words of discouragement had put a damper on Sam's joy at being with his kinfolk again, and he spent his last Sunday at home in a resentful mood.

He was pleased, however, to see that they had coped well enough in his absence. Young John was maturing quickly and had proved an able substitute. The piglet had turned into a fine porker and would provide the family with meat for a long time. A plenteous harvest of both oats and potatoes meant they would have a comfortable winter period, and of course Sam's financial contribution added gilt edged security to the well-being of the household.

It was the second Monday in September when he left to return to the canal and his lovely Teresa.

He made tentative promises to return at Christmas, but Seth's open hostility to a girl he'd never even met weighed heavily on his mind. If it came to a choice, Sam knew where his future lay.

Meanwhile at Preston Brook, Medlock was taking stock of the situation. Work was still continuing, albeit in a sporadic fashion. The kiln was at full capacity producing the huge stockpile of bricks necessary to lining the tunnel. Bridges were an essential too, to carry roads over the canal, and also enable farmers to gain access to their divided fields.

Large parts of the Trent and Mersey south of the tunnel were already complete and operational. This enabled the easy movement of vast supplies of clay, limestone and other materials to be brought almost to the south portal, from whence a string of pack horses transported them over the hill.

In the supervisor's office, Medlock and Peter Davies were engaging in some earnest conversations regarding the future.

'I reckon, George,' said Davies, 'the tunnel will be finished and open to traffic by next summer, so we'll be looking for a job elsewhere.'

'Ay, I suppose that's reet,' responded George, 'but there'll be plenty of work elsewhere along the cut, won't there?'

'Mebbe,' continued Davies, 'but the way I see it is like this.'

He pulled out a document and laid it on his desk.

'This is a copy of an Act of Parliament that allows for a branch line to be built at a place called Etruria. That's where Wedgwood has his potteries.'

'I've heard of that Wedgwood,' said George. 'Ain't he one of the bigwigs backing this whole concern?'

'He's a major shareholder, along with the Duke and others,' replied Davies. 'This branch line would give access to some big lime quarries near a place called Leek. They'll be looking for experienced men to dig it, and I reckon if you and I were to form our own little construction company, we could bid for one of the contracts.'

'A notion like that would tek a whole lot of money to get off the ground. Money I surely don't have,' said George.

'No more do I,' answered Davies, 'but it's my belief that we could set up a meeting with some local landowners and businessmen and suchlike to back us.'

'It sounds more than a bit chancy to me, Peter,' said George, 'never fancied mysen as a boss man.'

'You've nothing to lose, man!' cried Davies. 'This canal craze is sweeping the entire land and rich men are falling over themselves to get involved. You have a good set of lads with you and that stands us in good stead. All we need is £500 or so to get us the equipment we need.'

'It's a lot to tek in, Peter. Let me think on it a day or two.'

'Ay, George, but don't take too long about it. I'm telling you, this could make us our fortunes.'

So Medlock went away with much to occupy his mind.

He pondered long and hard on Davies' proposition and concluded that he had little to lose by joining him in the venture.

He hadn't forgotten his promise to Sam to watch over the young Irish lass, but so far nothing untoward had occurred.

He observed with pleasure the change that had come over the lovely Teresa. Gone was the forlorn, bewildered demeanour of bereavement. She seemed to glow with the exuberance of her newfound love for Sam.

* * *

Reilly was still very much an outcast in the camp and so kept his distance from everyone. He was still employed at the other end of the tunnel so George had little to do with him anyway.

The women of the camp were enjoying the leisure time afforded them by the reduced workload and took to accompanying Teresa on her evening strolls in the woods. They made a harvest of their own from the abundance of blackberries, damsons and crab apples in the hedgerows. They took them back and with some purloined sugar from the storehouse made delicious jams and jellies.

Medlock, pre-occupied somewhat with Davies' proposition, had let his attention slip enough for Reilly to chance his arm again. One night he trailed the three women into the wood. Teresa had spotted a particularly well laden bush and had wandered a little way from her companions. She was stretching up to reach an abundance of berries from high on the bush and didn't realise that Reilly had crept up behind her.

He seized her in a powerful grip and pushed her to the ground. She fell heavily face down, too winded and frightened to raise the alarm and he pounced on top of her and began to raise her skirts. He had already exposed his penis in readiness and with great excitement realised that the prize was his for the taking.

Such was his feverish excitement at the thought that at last this young beauty was finally at his mercy, he hadn't given a thought to the possibility of the other women coming to her aid.

However, the other two women, realising that Teresa had wandered off, heard the sounds of the scuffling in the bushes and came swiftly onto the scene.

The women had brought a heavy copper pan with them, which they left in one place, returning to it with handfuls of their wild fruit. It was already too heavy for one of them to lift alone but, driven to a fury by Reilly's actions, in unison they lifted it, swung it and with all their might smashed it down on the back of Reilly's head knocking him out stone cold.

They dragged his limp body away from his distressed victim. Whilst Annie did her best to comfort the horrified girl, Lizzie examined Reilly's blood-stained head. She could see no sign of him breathing.

'Oh, Jesus, Annie,' she gulped. 'I think we've done for him. He's not breathing.'

'Good enough for the bastard,' answered Annie tersely. 'He's done with attacking young girls at least.'

In the meantime, Medlock, still deep in thought as he made his rounds, became aware that there was no sign of Teresa. He noted that the other Irish ladies were also nowhere to be seen, but mindful of his promise he made his way into the wood to look for them.

At length, he came across the dramatic scene in the wood.

The sight of the three devastated women and the uncon-scious Reilly at their feet needed no explanation as to what had taken place. The overturned copper pan, smeared with blood and crushed blackberries, was proof enough.

He quickly took stock of the situation. Examining Reilly closely, he also could feel no pulse or sign of breathing.

'Don't distress thyselves unduly, ladies,' he advised. 'He was a worthless blaggard, and I doubt he'll be missed by anybody.'

He continued, 'Come now, back to the camp. Say nowt to anybody. I'll come back and give him a decent burial, though he hardly deserves it.'

He accompanied them through the woodland and back to the campsite.

The Docherty brothers had gone off to the harvest gatherings, but their cousin Gerard had opted to stay behind, so Medlock summoned him.

'Gerry, my man I need thy help. Bring two shovels and come with me.'

Mystified, Mulryan did as he was asked and as they went back to the grim scene, Medlock informed him of the reason for their mission and their gruesome task.

When they reached the scene of the shocking event, Medlock gasped in astonishment for there was no sign of Reilly.

'He must have come to,' Medlock surmised. 'We'll have to find him - he can't have gone far.'

'Jesus, gaffer, what the hell happened here?' asked Mulryan. 'I'm not too sure,' answered Medlock. 'Looks like he went after the young lass again, and either thy missus or t' other one, or more likely both of 'em, crowned him. He was not breathing when we came back for you, but the bugger must be built like a donkey. Reet, Gerry, best get searching.'

They soon found some spots of blood on the grass and began to follow the trail.

After an hour or so they still hadn't found their quarry, and with the autumn daylight rapidly diminishing decided to call off the hunt.

'We'll have to go back Gerry and get more men and have another look in the morning. God knows where the buggers got to,' said Medlock.

They made their way with some difficulty in the gathering gloom back to the base.

* * *

The three Irishwomen were still very subdued and shocked by the evening's events.

'Did you do what you said?' asked Lizzie anxiously.

'I'm sorry, lass,' replied George. 'There was no sign of him when we went back. He must have come to and staggered off.'

'Oh, God help me,' sobbed Teresa. 'I just know he'll come back.'

'Don't fret, lass,' said George, holding the trembling girl in a firm embrace. 'I don't think for one minute that he'll ever come back here, and even if he does, he has to get past me first.'

'If anybody starts asking questions,' he continued, 'none of you know nowt. He were a bad lot and like as not we've seen the back him.'

'Ay, surely, boss,' answered Mulryan. 'I don't think anybody's going to miss him. Just one more Paddy gone astray.'

'Come now, lasses,' said Medlock cheerily. 'Don't feel too down at what's 'appened. He were an all-round troublemaker. Best cheer thyselves up or some might think tha knows summat.'

He took them to his own little hut and gave them all a nip of brandy, which did the trick to some extent.

Teresa, despite the warm glow of the fiery liquid, was still shaking from the ordeal. She spent the night snuggled close to Annie in her tent, and despite everything was soon sleeping soundly.

George and Gerry decided that it would be prudent to mount a guard of the women folk and took two-hour turns through the night.

Thankfully, despite a more thorough search the next morning, no trace of the evil Reilly was found.

* * *

Sometime after the departure of Medlock and the women, Reilly came round. Although dazed and shaken with a very sore head, he took stock of his situation. He realised that his lustful and cynical treatment of womenkind had landed him in deep trouble once more.

He'd never be able to return to the dig again, and despite the considerable wages and bonus owing to him, he decided to cut his losses and head south.

He also was acutely aware that a search party might come after him, and so he staggered away from the scene.

Despite his aching head he knew he must put as much distance between himself and the canal as soon as he could and hope for the darkness to swallow him up. He found a spot where he could crawl into the undergrowth and spent a restless night with only the woodland creatures for company.

Tom Reilly managed his escape and went on his way, finding work where he could. Robbing travellers when he was short of funds, and assaulting women when his lustful desires got the better of him.

He ended his days a few years later dancing a jig between Heaven and Hell on the end of a rope in Stafford jail.

Chapter Twenty

Sam made an early start on the Monday morning, having a full day's ride in front of him. There was much embracing and quite a few tears as he bade them all farewell, but as much as he knew he would miss his family, he was eager to get back to Preston Brook and the sweetheart who'd given his life new meaning.

He was still feeling aggrieved at his father's unfair appraisal of Teresa but had kept his feelings to himself when they parted. He resolved to try to bring her with him if he ever got the chance to return home again, He hoped that when Seth met his darling Tess in the flesh his ill-founded prejudices would melt away, but whether or when that might happen was impossible to envision.

The late summer days were getting shorter, and it was almost dusk by the time he arrived back at the camp. The communal dining area was a welcome sight, with candles already lighting the gloom and the aroma of the huge pots of broth simmering away on the hearth.

He was made welcome by the assembly of men and the serving women but was disconcerted to see that Teresa was nowhere to be seen.

'Don't fret, boy,' chortled Annie, 'she's only gone to the store for some salt. She'll get a surprise when she sees ye.'

Sure enough, presently, the young lass returned to the food hut and gasped audibly at the sight of her returning hero. She rushed to his arms and, to the cheers of the whole assembly, Sam folded her in his strong embrace.

Despite the long day's ride and his empty stomach, Sam's only thought was to take his girl to where they'd have a little more privacy, and so they stumbled out into the gathering dusk and made their way towards the general storehouse. They sat on a rough-hewn bench that the sawyers had made and fervently made up for the weeks of separation with long breathless kisses.

Sam already knew instinctively that he'd found his life partner and lost no time in telling her so.

'Oh, my dearest sweetest treasure,' he murmured. 'Never let us be parted again.'

He sank to his knees before her and taking her hands in his he uttered the time-honoured phrase.

'Will you be my bride? You'll never want for aught in your whole life.'

Sam was perturbed when she made no immediate response. He looked up earnestly at her stricken face.

'Oh Sam,' she sobbed tearfully. 'That cannot ever be. There are certain things that make that an impossible dream.'

'Tess, my darling, what on earth could come between us. If it's your religion, I care nothing for it,' he declared. 'Why should the church thwart a match made in Heaven?'

'No, my darling, it's not that. I care not a whit for the church. There are things that you don't know, that would change your mind about me, and I can't speak of them.'

Sam replied, 'Tess, you're the loveliest creature I've ever met, and nothing in your past could deter me from wanting you as my wife.'

'Oh, Sam,' she sobbed. 'It's no good. It just cannot be!'

With that, she arose and ran back to her tent, leaving the poor lad in a state of perplexed misery and confusion. Despondently he made his way back to the dining hall, but despite his hunger could only manage a few spoonfuls of the nourishing bowl that was put before him.

He trudged wearily to his sleeping quarters, but found he could not lose himself in slumber, wondering what on earth was this massive obstacle that had shattered his dreams.

True, he knew nothing of her past, or her relationship with poor young Will. In his headlong tumble into love of the wistful creature, he'd never thought to question from whence she came, other than that she was just one more young lass who'd managed to escape the poverty of her native land.

The following day dawned chilly and grey to match Sam's mood. He joined Medlock and the rest of the men on the walk back to the tunnel.

In their absence a substantial length of the roof of the cavity had been brick-lined, which seemed to add a sense of purpose to the work of excavation, and for the most part they set about their digging with renewed vigour. Sam threw himself furiously into his work to the amused concern of the others of the gang.

'Jesus, Sam will ye slow down!' remarked Tom Docherty. 'Save thy energy for that sweet lass of yours.'

Sam, flushed with rage, threw down his shovel and went for Docherty in a blind fury.

It took a great effort from Medlock, Gerry and Matt to drag him away before he did Tom any serious damage.

Medlock drew him well away from the others and holding him in a fierce grip said, 'What in Christ's name has got into thee lad?'

The youngster's rage slowly abated, and he stammered out an apology.

'Don't tell me, boy,' shouted Medlock. 'I've never had trouble between my lads before. It's Tom ye've to mek it up with, so get on with it or ye're done here.'

Meekly, Sam did as he was bid and went over to Tom who was none the worse for Sam's onslaught.

'Sorry Tom,' he said, offering his hand. 'You hit a raw spot and I lost my head.'

'Ay, all right, boy,' answered Tom affably, 'I didn't mean to speak out of turn. ''ll keep my big gob shut in future.'

They resumed their morning labours with an inevitable air of tension and there was a palpable relief when Medlock announced the down tools for the mid-day meal break.

As usual the women had brought their food in a large pot and busied themselves serving their menfolk. Sam looked for Teresa, but she was nowhere to be seen.

Lizzie called him to one side and whispered, 'Sam, I don't know what's passed between ye, but she's breaking her heart and we can do nothing to comfort her.'

Medlock was shrewdly observing this fierce whispering, and came over to Sam and said bluntly, 'Tha'll be no good in t' tunnel, 'til ye get matters put reet lad. Be off with ye, and do what ye have to do.'

Sam needed no second bidding and at took off at a brisk pace along the towpath. When he arrived, Teresa was nowhere to be seen. There were very few people around at this time of day, but Mr. Davies was standing in the doorway off his office.

'What are you doing back here at this time,' he demanded. 'Are ye injured, lad?'

'No sir,' answered Sam. 'It's a personal matter.'

'Ah, if it concerns a certain young lass, she took herself off a while ago,' said Davies. 'Be quick about your business or I'll have to dock your pay.'

Sam instinctively guessed where he'd find her and set off into the woods. Sure enough, he found her sitting on the fallen log that she seemed to have adopted as her own private resting place.

He made no attempt to disguise his approach and strode straight into the clearing and stood in front of her.

'Tess, if you can't or won't tell me of this terrible hindrance between us, I'm going back to my kinfolk. I'll not stay here without you.'

'You'll want nothing more to do with me, if I tell you,' she whimpered. 'I do love you, but I'm not worthy of your love.'

'Why won't you let me make my own judgment?' he implored her. 'I'm sure nothing could change my feelings for you.'

He knelt in front of her and took her hands in his. 'I'll always love you no matter what. Nothing or no-one could alter that.'

After what to Sam seemed an agonisingly long time, Teresa swallowed hard and in a quavering voice said 'Well, for one thing my name isn't Teresa, it's Mary - Mary O'Farrell. Poor Will too - he was really called Joe Molloy. We sought to cover ourselves with a change of name.'

* * *

Bit by bit she recounted the whole story of their flight from the clutches of the despotic Regan. Young Joe was just a loyal and true friend with every reason to join her in her flight to freedom.

Sam let her tell her story without interruption, in awe at the sheer bravery of the epic journey that the two young Irish adolescents had undertaken.

She'd faltered a little when admitting that Regan had stolen her innocence and used her over and over. The theft of his horse, money and watch was something else she was loath to admit, but realised that she could hold nothing back if she wanted peace of mind.

Reaching the end of her confession she sobbed, 'So you see my lovely man, that I am naught but a fallen woman and a common thief, with a hangman's rope to face if they ever find me.'

Sam sat beside her in silence for a while. He put his arm around her and let her bury her head against his chest crying softly.

'Everything you've told me alters nothing,' he said eventually. 'Indeed, I'm filled with wonder at your bravery.'

'My darling Tess,' he continued, 'Mary belongs in the past, and no-one knows of her but we two. Ye'll always be Tess to me, and I'll not rest until you become Mrs Teresa Burton.'

'Oh Sam,' she gasped. 'Can this really happen? What of your kinfolk? Surely, they won't want a common Irish trollop for a daughter.'

'Ye can let me take care of that,' answered Sam. 'Gone are the days when my father tells me what to do!'

* * *

They ambled back to the camp with the air of complete rapture, safe and secure in their love. The confusion and doubts swept aside for all time.

However, they were swiftly brought back to earth by the stern countenance of Mr. Davies.

'Now, young man, I can tell that whatever ailed ye both has been put right,' he said. 'So ye'd better get back to the dig with all haste.'

'I will right away, sir, and thank you for your patience,' answered Sam.

'Off ye go then,' he said smiling warmly. Turning to Teresa he added, 'God bless you, girl, you've found a good lad there.'

So Sam, with a new spring in his step, marched back to the camaraderie and gentle teasing of his workmates.

Chapter Twenty-One

Days were turning into weeks of fruitless enquiries for Fintan Regan. It seemed that no-one knew anything of the young fugitives. So many itinerants were seeking work in the thriving town or passing through on the road to Manchester and beyond. It really was like looking for a needle in a hayrick.

However, the relationship between father and son was growing into an ever-stronger bond of mutual affection.

Henry was starting to lose his inhibitions, gradually becoming accustomed to his new station in life.

Fintan for his part was relishing his new outlook and played the role of doting father to the uttermost.

It was the last week in October when a coincidence happened that was to have a profound effect on many lives.

Regan had reached a point of frustrated despair and was already making plans to call off this futile search and return to Wexford before the dead of winter.

He'd been showering his son with lavish gifts of fine clothes, books and items of jewellery. As they were passing a shop displaying all manner of gentleman's clothing and accessories one morning, Henry saw on display in the window a rather handsome watch and chain.

He'd been told by his indulgent father to ask for anything that took his fancy, so they entered the shop and asked to see the watch.

The proprietor, Mr. Arnold Beasley, only too anxious to please, placed the item into the young man's hand with the words, 'Tis a fine piece, young sir, solid gold as you can see. Feel the weight. Normally it would sell at 12 guineas, but as it has already been inscribed on the back, I can let you have it for ten.'

Henry handed the watch to his father, 'It's wonderful. Do you think I might have it?'

Regan examined the said piece and was shaken to the very core of his being. He realised immediately that it was the very one stolen from him all those weeks ago. The initials F R and the date 1771 were all the confirmation he needed.

Shrewdly, he held back from accusing Beasley, not wanting to put the man on his guard.

'Of course, you may have it, son,' he said levelly, trying to hide the elation in his voice.

He counted out the ten coins into Beasley's hand, who duly fixed the watch to Henry's handsome waistcoat.

'A fine adornment for a handsome young man,' he crowed.

His elation quickly changed to one of alarm when Regan stepped in front of him with a menacing look on his face.

'Now my man,' growled Regan. 'You can tell me when and how you acquired this piece.'

Beasley became flustered and began to tremble in fear. 'I can't rightly remember from whence it came,' he spluttered.

'Well, I suggest you'd better start remembering, and do so in haste,' retorted Regan.

'What is it to you, anyway?' said Beasley, recovering his composure somewhat. 'I bought it in good faith and have sold it to you in equal measure.'

'My good sir,' countered Regan. 'This very watch was stolen from me in Ireland in the month of June. I can easily prove this to be true. I can send for the magistrate and constable, if that's your desire?'

'Now look here,' blustered Beasley. 'Anyone can come here and make such a claim. Give me back the watch and I'll return your money and be off with you.'

'If that is how you wish to deal with the matter, so be it,' answered Regan. 'We'll keep the watch, thank you, and I shall attend the magistrate with the bill of sale from Lynch's of Dublin - the world-renowned jewellers. I'm sure you'll be aware of the offence of receiving stolen goods?'

This last claim was a tremendous piece of bluff. Such a bill did exist, but it was hundreds of miles away in Dunslaney.

However, the ploy worked well, for Beasley began to panic again and said, 'Wait there, sir. I'll see if I can find the relevant paper.'

He made a pretext of searching in a large wooden desk that stood at the back of the shop. No such paper did he possess, but the pretence gave him some time to consider his options.

He knew well enough who had sold him the watch. Mrs Kelly had supplied other items of dubious ancestry in the past. He was loath to give her away but realised that to divert attention from himself he had little choice.

'Ah, I have it!' he exclaimed exultantly. 'It was brought here by a Mrs Kelly, who I believe has a lodging house in the dock area.'

'And the address?' asked Regan gruffly.

'That, sir I'm afraid I do not know' said Beasley. 'I did not think to ask her at the time.'

Regan snatched the paper, which was actually completely blank, from Beasley's hand.

'Yet more fudge, ye old scoundrel,' he thundered. 'By God I'll have the truth from you sir before I leave this place!'

Beasley scurried back behind the huge desk vainly seeking a refuge.

'I speak the truth. I know not where she resides, only that it must be a large dwelling near the quayside.'

'If you are at last being truthful, which I much doubt, I suppose I'll have to search for myself. But if I don't find her, I'll be back. You can be assured of that. Come Henry, we have work to do.'

With that, he swept imperiously from the shop with his astounded son behind him.

They returned to The Red Lion and partook of coffee in the comfortable surrounds of the lounge. Regan asked the desk clerk Edward Dunn to join them.

A tall thin man in his early forties with a hook nose on which perched a pair of pince-nez, he carried out his duties with great efficiency. Regan had observed him thus and had no doubt that Dunn would be a useful cohort in the search.

'Now sir,' Regan addressed the clerk. 'I can tell that you're the sort of man with his ear close to the ground. Have ye heard tell of a woman named Kelly who runs a lodging house hereabouts?'

'Oh yes indeed, Mr Regan,' he replied eagerly. 'She's an Irishwoman from Dublin, I believe. I've heard she has a respectable home where she welcomes her fellow countrymen mostly.'

'Will you take me there?' asked Regan.

'I'm afraid that's not possible just at the moment, sir. I have my duties to attend to here,' replied Dunn.

'Come man, surely you can be spared for an hour? I'll make it worth your while.'

Regan produced a couple of sovereigns, which Dunn, with little hesitation, pocketed adroitly. He called young Charles Varney, a potboy, over and told him to mind the desk for a while.

To his son, Regan said, 'Stay here Henry and keep that young man company. If anyone asks, Mr Dunn has urgent business that could not wait. By the way, I need to borrow your new watch.'

Henry, although reluctant to be parted from his new possession or to miss the forthcoming encounter, knew better than to question his father, so did as he was bid.

The two men set off at a brisk pace towards the quayside district.

'I'm not entirely sure of the location,' said Dunn, 'but it must be in this vicinity.'

Mid-day was almost upon them and the whole area was swarming with dock workers and carriers. Laden wagons journeyed to and fro between the two large ships moored at the quay. Dunn took the initiative and asked a couple of the wharf-men with strong Irish accents if they knew of Mrs Kelly.

It was a shrewd move because both of the Irishmen had stayed at her house in Stanley Street at one time and pointed the searchers in the right direction.

They found the lodging house without too much trouble and Regan dismissed Dunn. 'Thank you for your assistance my friend,' said Regan. 'I can attend to this matter myself now, so it would be better for you to return to your work.'

'I'm glad to have been able to help, sir,' answered a very relieved Dunn. 'If I can be of use to you again don't hesitate to ask.'

With that Dunn made off and Regan rapped hard on the door.

When Kitty opened the door and saw a fine gentleman, she was immediately on her guard.

'What can I do for you sir?' she asked cautiously.

'I presume you are Mrs Kelly?' said Regan.

'Yes, that is my name,' she answered warily.

'I have good reason to believe that you know of the whereabouts of two young Irish people - a lad and a lass who arrived here some time ago,' continued Regan, fixing her with a steely glance.

'So many of my countrymen and women pass this way seeking lodgings' retorted Kitty. 'I can't be expected to recall every one of them.'

'Think carefully, madam, or you may find yourself in serious trouble,' warned Regan.

'I have nothing to tell you, fine sir, so please be on your way.'

Kitty tried to slam the door in his face, but Regan was too quick for her and pushed past her into the hall.

'You'd better heed what I say, Mrs Kelly,' he said gravely. 'I have no intention of leaving here without the information that I know you possess.'

* * *

He withdrew the watch from his pocket and dangled it in front of the startled woman.

'I know that you sold this watch to that old rogue Beasley,' he said. 'It's the very one that was stolen from me weeks ago in Wexford, so don't try to deny it.'

'I bought it in all honesty from a young couple who were in my debt,' jabbered Kitty defensively.

'This much, I already know,' responded Regan, and in a softer tone continued, 'look woman, I need to know of their whereabouts. Despite their thieving ways, I want nothing more than to bring Joseph and Mary home to Wexford with me and to right the wrongs that have been done to them.'

'Ah then!' exclaimed Kitty exultantly. 'You're making a big mistake, for their names were Will and Teresa, and they hailed from County Galway.'

Regan pondered this new attestation for a few moments and then countered, 'I can only surmise that they gave false names to cover their tracks, but they are undoubtedly the pair that I seek. The watch is definitely mine, and what's more, the lad Joe was almost apprehended at the dockside some weeks ago. Indeed, that is the very reason that I have trailed them to this town.'

'I know nothing more,' said Kitty. 'I gave them money for the watch to cover the cost of their stay with me. They set off for Manchester weeks and weeks ago. That's all I have to say, so kindly leave me in peace sir.'

'You know for certain that Manchester was their destination?' Regan persisted.

'So many of our countrymen pass through here trying to find a better life than you and your like offer them in their homeland,' answered Kitty, defiantly. 'All I can give them is a place to lay their heads 'til they find their feet. Manchester is where they usually make for after leaving here, but some of them maybe try for work on this new-fangled canal that's being dug.'

'Thank you, madam, for what little you've given me,' said Regan. 'I'm certain you know more than you're telling me, and I may well return to question you further. Receiving stolen property is a serious offence so I would search my memory diligently if I were you.'

He turned on his heel and headed for the door, but before leaving added, 'Can you not see that it would be in your best interest to help me. I repeat, I mean the young people no harm. In fact, young Joe stands to gain massively from returning to Ireland. As for Mary, when I find her, as I surely will, I intend to marry her, if she'll have me.'

He returned to the Red Lion to tell Henry and Dunn of his findings. Dunn was able to provide more useful information, regarding the canal.

'I believe that the canal Mrs Kelly is alluding to is called the Grand Junction,' he said in his usual measured tone. When complete it is supposed to link the Mersey with the Trent. It is a mighty undertaking, and many hundreds of workers from all over the kingdom are employed on it.'

'So, it's quite possible that the two runaways could have made their way there?' pondered Regan.

'Ay, 'tis more than likely, I'd say,' replied Dunn. 'It's not as far as Manchester and they'd surely find work there.'

The following morning, Regan, with young Henry in tow, returned to Mrs Kelly and rapped on the door.

'I hope you've given some serious thought to what I said yesterday, Madam,' he said. 'I have no wish to bring the law down upon you, but you must realise the sincerity of my quest.'

Kitty had indeed spent a largely sleepless night worrying about what might befall her. She wished heartily that she'd never seen the cursed watch or been foolish enough to buy it. She'd been through enough hardship of her own in the past. This prosperous little business that she's striven hard for could be snatched from her if she didn't co-operate. On the other hand, she was loath to put Regan on the trail of the fugitives despite his avowal of his altruistic intentions.

Actually, Regan's decision to bring Henry along with him was a wise one. He explained that young Henry had also been wronged in the past and that he was doing everything he could to make up for his earlier indifference to his own flesh and blood.

So impressed was Kitty by the obvious love and affection between father and son that she decided that Regan was genuine. She decided it was time to come clean and get herself off the hook.

'Well, sir,' she began, 'I'll tell ye all I know. I did indeed advise them to try for the canal rather than seek their fortune in Manchester, and as far as I know that is where they intended to go when they left here.'

'How long since they left?' asked Regan.

'I'm not rightly sure,' answered Kitty. 'It was some weeks ago.'

'How would I get there?'

'You have to find your way to the Duke's cut first, which is just a few miles from here. I'm sure you'd find someone to lead you there.'

'Are you positive that there's nothing more ye have to tell me?' asked Regan, desperate for any slight detail that might aid his quest.

'I can only add that you need to find a place called Preston Brook. I understand that's where the new canal joins the Duke's.'

Thanking her for her co-operation, Regan and Henry returned to the Red Lion to make plans for the next stage of the quest.

In the spacious lounge he once again enlisted the services of the admirable Edward Dunn.

'Have ye heard of this place Preston Brook?' Regan enquired.

'Oh, yes sir,' replied Dunn. ''Tis a small village a few miles hence, and I believe 'tis where the two canals join together.'

'Good man. Now what would be the best way for us to get there?' continued Regan.

'I would suggest on horseback sir, across country, for the road is very poor and probably beset with robbers and the like.'

'Mr Dunn, would you be able to procure good horses for us?' asked Regan, once again producing guineas from his purse.

'Thank you, sir. I'll make enquiries,' said Dunn, accepting the coins with deference. 'When would you like them to be brought here?'

'I think I shall need several days, in which to make proper preparation,' replied Regan. 'Tell me, is there an armourer in this town? I'll need a small-sword or rapier for protection.'

'I believe a Mr Humphrey Cowley has the premises you seek, sir, in the High Street.'

'Mr Dunn, you are a Godsend!' exclaimed Regan. 'Your service to me will not be forgotten.'

* * *

Over the course of the next few days, Regan and son equipped themselves, not only with weaponry, but greatcoats and good strong boots. The weather was turning very autumnal with long spells of heavy rain and buffeting winds.

Although given to act on impulse at times, Regan also had periods of deep rational reasoning. His admiration and respect for the efficiency of Dunn, despite the latter's dour demeanour, had brought him to the conclusion that his services could prove invaluable on a permanent basis.

On the very next evening, with his plans for the mission very much underway, he summoned Dunn to his presence in a private room at the back of the inn.

'Mr Dunn, or Edward if I may so address you,' began Regan, 'I have a proposition to put before you. I have been most impressed by the efficient manner in which you conduct the business of this establishment and your personal assistance to me.'

'I am thankful to have been able to give such assistance to you sir,' replied Dunn.

'Well,' continued Regan, 'as you may have gathered, I am a man of considerable wealth and property back in Ireland and I find myself in need of a personal assistant, or secretary if you prefer, to organise my affairs. I would like to offer you the post.'

Dunn of course, was absolutely thrown by this proposition. He tried to recover his composure by going around the room tidying things and re-arranging some of the furniture.

At length, he answered in his usual calm manner, 'You have taken me completely by surprise, sir. I'm very flattered by the suggestion but would need time to consider it fully.'

'By all means take your time, Edward,' rejoined Regan. 'The position is a new one and will carry a salary of £150 per annum with all living expenses in addition.'

'It would entail for me a mighty upheaval, sir - I have never journeyed beyond Liverpool in my life,' said Dunn.

'Well, as I have said,' continued Regan, 'I know it will be a big decision for you to make, but life at Dunslaney is not so very different from a grand English house, and I'm sure you would soon settle in.'

'May I take the rest of today to consider your offer sir and give you my answer in the morning?' replied Dunn.

'But of course, my dear fellow,' said Regan. 'I think you and I would work very well together. I have significant plans for my estate and affairs when I return, and I can see in you just the sort of man I need to help me carry them through.'

Dunn went back to his own quarters, and over his simple frugal supper began to evaluate the momentous offer that he'd received.

He was a single man. His parents were both deceased and his only living relative was his married sister, Rosalind in Liverpool.

Regan was offering a salary far in excess of his present one. In his methodical manner he weighed up the pros and cons of the proposal. The only major doubt in his mind was the prospect of what life in Ireland would entail.

Like most Englishmen, his only knowledge of the country was based on hearsay and travellers' gossip. He understood it to be a land inhabited by ignorant starving peasantry, trodden underfoot by a class of privileged gentry of which his prospective employer was a prominent member.

He'd reached the age of forty-three and by diligence and self-discipline had attained enough education to consider himself something of an expert in accounting and man management.

After hours of deliberation lasting well into the night, he did his final round of checking that the Red Lion was running smoothly and waiting patiently for the last of the drinkers to leave. There were at present only one traveller and the Regans in accommodation, so he closed and locked the premises and reached a decision. He would hand in his notice to the proprietor James Griffiths and throw in his lot with Regan. An abstemious man usually, he partook of a large glass of brandy in celebration and slept soundly.

* * *

The following morning, he was confronted by Regan who was anxious to know if his offer had been accepted.

'I have made my decision, sir,' announced Dunn, 'and I would like to accept your offer.'

'Good man!' exclaimed Regan enthusiastically. 'Let us shake hands, you'll not regret it.'

'I will have to serve my notice here, sir. It should be four weeks. However, if I can find a worthy successor it may be possible to shorten the term.'

'I have no doubt that you will be successful in that endeavour, as with everything else you do,' said Regan. 'Now, as befits our new relationship, I'm going to tell you the full story of my mission here.'

'I have things to attend to at present sir,' said Dunn. 'But give me an hour or so and I will return.'

Sure enough before the hour was up, Regan and Dunn were ensconced in the same private room and Regan's lengthy discourse began. He told Dunn something of his early care-free life and how he'd enjoyed his pick of the local wenches, discarding them at will, until Mary had come along and shaken him to his very core. He went on to tell of the shocking revelation that the stable lad Joe was actually his half-brother, and the remarkable metamorphosis that he'd undergone when hearing of it.

He stressed to Dunn that his sense of remorse had completely changed his outlook on life and that his present mission was to make amends for the suffering that the actions of himself and his forebears had committed. He was under no illusion as to the formidable nature of the quest that he'd embarked upon but would have no peace until he'd done all in his power to find the wronged youngsters. He went on to explain how young Henry had also been the victim of a great injustice. That was why he was determined to make up for lost time and lavish such love and care on his newly found son.

Dunn listened intently to this discourse without interruption and when Regan had finished, he intertwined his long bony fingers together and spoke thus, 'Tis a remarkable tale, sir, and a noble mission. I only hope that you find the success it surely deserves. However, you must face the possibility, nay even the probability of failure.'

'This thought has caused me many a sleepless night,' answered Regan. 'I shall find no peace, however, until I have resolved the matter for better or worse.'

Ever the practical, Dunn proposed that Regan should forthwith seek a lawyer to draw up appropriate documentation to legalise these weighty matters, and that the final stage of his search must be postponed until such formalities were completed.

'You're right, of course, Edward,' said Regan. 'Do you know of a reputable man of letters?'

'The person you seek sir is one, Arthur Linnett,' replied Dunn. 'I know him to be an honest upright citizen of this town well able to be of service to you.'

'Please arrange an appointment for me, forthwith,' said Regan. 'The days are growing shorter, and I really hope to settle things before the year's end.'

Mindful of his new status, Dunn lost no time in contacting and procuring the services of the solicitor, Linnet. He explained the nature of his employer's requirements and Linnett, recognising a lucrative piece of business when he saw it, immediately got to work on the project.

The resulting documents were produced with considerable alacrity and three days later, towards the end of November, Regan was summoned to Linnet's office to sign several documents, including a new will, making Joseph Molloy and Henry his joint heirs, and a comprehensive contract of employment for Dunn.

Satisfied that all legal matters had been taken care of as far as was feasible, Regan turned back to the preparation for the journey.

Dunn had thought it advisable for the travellers to select their own steeds in person and so led them to Warlands livery stable to do so.

Regan picked two fine looking specimens - a sixteen-hand black stallion named Bullet and a fourteen-hand chestnut filly called Nutmeg for Henry - and ordered them to be brought to the Red Lion in two days hence.

This stable, of course, was the very place where young Will had been employed before his near capture. Capricious fate had dealt the blow that was to cost him his life, although Regan and Henry were of course blissfully unaware of that tragic irony.

They returned to their quarters to make their final arrangements.

Chapter Twenty-Two

At Preston Brook work on the tunnel had continued apace without too much disruption, until the days grew shorter and the weather began to deteriorate.

Heavy, persistent rain fell for three days in early November, turning the whole site into a muddy morass, severely hindering progress.

In the tunnel itself some work was still possible, but it was an exhausting, energy sapping affair. Despite the heavy labour of constant digging and shovelling, the men were soon numb with cold in the dark damp defines of their surrounds.

The journey back to the camp was itself a debilitating footslog through the mud. The only comfort was the fact that the weekly bath had become a nightly affair much to be looked forward too.

Bradshaw and Davies, with great acumen, realised that the workers needed better accommodation if they were going to endure the winter that lay ahead. There was an abundant supply of timber and other materials to hand. Work on the canal was severely hampered by the weather, so the men were put to work building proper warm shelter for themselves.

Within a few days, a hastily built but adequate number of large dormitories began to take shape. The workforce applied themselves with great diligence, realising that the sooner the task was completed, the greater their collective comfort to face the winter.

The appalling conditions however, had done nothing to dilute the blossoming love of the two young sweethearts, and their plans for a swift marriage before the year was out.

Teresa's faith might have proved a stumbling block if the wedding was to take place in a church, but that was a formality they were willing to bypass.

Sam turned to Medlock and Davies for advice.

'Is it lawful to marry outside of the church, George?' asked Sam.

'Don't reetly know,' replied Medlock. 'All I can say on t' subject is if ye're fond enough of each other, what does it matter if it don't 'appen in church?'

'I'd go ahead, lad,' offered Davies. 'Nobody here will challenge it, of that I'm damned sure. Do you have a ring for the lass?'

'No sir,' responded Sam. 'But I have money saved to get one.'

'Just hold on,' said Davies, disappearing into his office.

He returned a moment later and handed Sam a gold wedding ring.

'I'd say that'd fit the lass, more or less, wouldn't you?' He added, 'Twas my mother's, and I couldn't think of a better home for it.'

'Oh, Mr Davies,' gasped Sam. 'Please let me pay you something for it.'

'No, my boy,' responded Davies. 'You keep your money, 'tis my gift to you to help you on your way.'

* * *

For young Mary O'Farrell of Wexford, it had been the most tumultuous year of her life.

The loss of her entire family, followed by her violation at the hands of a ruthless master would be enough for any young maid of seventeen summers to bear. She was still grieving for the loss of tragic young Joe Molloy, despite her all-consuming love of her handsome young hero, Sam.

Now she was on the brink of another huge threshold and she was full of trepidation for whatever the fates might still have in store for her. She could hardly believe it was all actually happening. At the back of her mind was the lingering fear that yet another disaster would come along to dash her hopes once again.

There was to be no time however, to let these doubts and fears prey too heavily on her mind, for Sam had suggested that there was no need to postpone their happy day and she readily agreed.

On a frosty Sunday morning in mid-November the young lovers were joined together.

It was, inevitably, an informal arrangement. Peter Davies had drawn up an official looking document, which would probably not have stood up in a court of law. He then performed a perfunctory ceremony with some words borrowed from the Anglican marriage service. Some of the women from the village had made a rudimentary bridal gown and veil for Mary.

George Medlock 'gave the bride away'. Sam placed the ring on her finger, albeit a little loosely, and to great joy all round Sam and Teresa became man and wife.

The usual week-end feast of roast meat and vegetables became the wedding breakfast, and the celebrations went on well into the dark autumn night.

The bride and groom stole away sometime during the festivities to the hut they'd been allocated where, after a few preliminary nerves, they consummated their union with a joyful passion.

* * *

The following morning the newlyweds emerged from the "bridal suite" to a greeting of cheers and good-natured bantering, causing them both to blush profusely.

After a hearty breakfast it was back to the endless slog of the tunnel for Sam and his work mates.

The weather had entered a cold and frosty phase, which at least dried the ground a little and so inch by miserable inch the tunnellers hacked their way toward one another. The gang working at the bottom of the shaft had the more arduous task. It was still only possible for two men to work at the face of the dig, whilst others were engaged on removing the spoil and loading it in the pannier to be hauled to the surface.

The tons of earth and rock were then taken by pack horse to the southern end of the tunnel, and from there loaded onto barges to be taken on the completed section of the canal to various locations for use on embankments and other earthworks.

The other gang, working inward from the tunnel entrance, were somewhat relieved at the knowledge that behind them the tunnel was being shored up, giving some sense of security, however dubious.

Despite the appalling working conditions, the work-force had to endure their lot - there was no such thing as bad weather compensation. Work or starve were the only stark alternatives.

There were times when the digging was completely impossible and on such days the workforce were kept busy. Bricks to be made, timbers to be cut and all manner of other menial tasks to ensure there was still gainful employment to be had.

For the newlyweds, life was blissfully happy despite the wretchedness of the environment and winter weather. Every night Sam would return weary and mud stained to the welcome tub of hot water that Teresa would have waiting. After the usual pottage of broth and huge slabs of bread, he'd retire to the marriage bed and the loving arms of his adoring young bride.

They knew nothing of the dramatic events that were about to unfold and shape their future.

Chapter Twenty-Three

Now that he was about to embark upon the final part of his quest, Fintan became troubled by the thought that the journey and subsequent hoped-for rendezvous might be too much for his son to undertake.

Since Edward Dunn was now in his employ, a solution to his dilemma became apparent.

In their bedchamber on the night before the intended journey was to begin, he sat down beside his son and announced 'Henry, my boy, I have given much thought to the arduous nature of the mission ahead and I've a mind to leave you here in the care of Mr. Dunn.'

'Oh, please no, father,' answered Henry with great consternation. 'I beg you please let me ride with you. I won't be a hindrance.'

'No, as I have said, much deliberation has gone into my decision. I have no idea of what lies ahead or how long it will take me to achieve my objective. I have made up my mind that you must stay here and await my return.'

The troubled boy began to sniffle.

'Come sir,' said Regan sternly. 'This is no way for a young gentleman to behave. You'll be perfectly well cared for here. Mr. Dunn will, I have no doubt, see to your every need. I have made a financial arrangement to cater for your board and keep for the time being. By the grace of God, the outcome will be decided before too long.'

There was a knock at the door and Dunn entered.

'Henry,' said Regan. 'Mr Dunn has been offered and has accepted the position of my personal secretary and, from now until my return, will be your mentor and guardian.'

'Don't worry, young sir,' said Dunn, putting a friendly arm around the boy's shoulders.

Henry flinched, jumped up and ran from the room shouting, 'It's not fair, it's damnable.'

Dunn went to follow him, but Regan shook his head and said, 'Leave him, Edward. He's suffered a disappointment - let him go, he'll return soon enough. Find something to occupy his mind whilst I'm away.'

'I have to work my notice here,' replied Dunn. 'I'll give him some accounting and the like to fill his time.'

'Ay, that's an excellent notion. It'll do him no harm to learn the rudiments of bookkeeping,' remarked Regan. 'The business that I'm engaged on might prove quite a hazardous operation, the outcome of which I cannot be sure of. Look after my boy. He's very dear to me.'

'Have no fear on that score,' said Dunn. 'I'm sure he and I will be the best of friends by the time you return sir.'

Young Henry spent a restless night. He had soon got over his dismay at his father's decision. He was still very much in awe of the man who'd changed his life so dramatically. He knew that he would have to abide by his father's wishes, but was full of fear of being left in the company of a man he scarcely knew in the strange new environment of an English town.

When they had embarked on this wild escapade, he had always doubted, with foresight beyond his young years, that his father's ambitions would be easily realised. He could see the mission ending in abject failure.

The fortunate finding of the watch has given fresh impetus to his father's endeavours, but it still seemed to young Henry that success was a faint prospect.

How on earth had his father convinced himself that he would find the fugitives - they might not have even reached the canal. A multitude of mishaps may have thwarted them. If, by some miracle, he managed to find them, convincing them to return with him would by no means be a foregone conclusion. He wished he had the confidence and assuredness to put these thoughts to his father, but the memory of his previous life as a lowly footman was still a huge part of his persona and he vowed to keep his own counsel.

Regan, for his part, had harboured many of the same doubts and fears, but was driven by a steely resolve to see the matter through no matter what the outcome.

His Damascus-like conversion from debauchery to earnest responsibility was still maturing. He knew he wouldn't feel fulfilled until he'd found that poor maiden and offered a sincere apology for using her so badly and proposed making an honest woman of her. As for young Joseph, Regan eagerly anticipated the joy of revealing to the lad his true status.

He was under no illusion about the enormity of his task, but the firm belief that it was the only way for his remorse to be assuaged drove him onward.

On the very last day of November - a bitingly cold, bright morning - Fintan Regan set off to find Preston Brook.

Over breakfast he'd discoursed at length with his son about the virtue of making the journey alone, trying to reassure the lad that he would be perfectly comfortable in the care of Dunn.

Dunn had agreed with Griffiths, the proprietor of The Red Lion, to stay in his post until Regan returned, as a suitable replacement manager was still to be found.

Father and son embraced fondly in the courtyard, and then Regan was gone without a backward glance.

He rode at a canter down the main thoroughfare, Bridge Street, until he reached the dockside. Crossing the Mersey via the bridge, he soon found himself in open country.

Dunn had produced a rudimentary map, which although by no means perfectly accurate, did at least keep him heading in the right direction.

All morning he maintained an easy canter though open farmland interspersed with small spinneys and copses. The weather remained cold, and the bright low sun became dazzling in its trajectory across the western sky. He kept a wary eye out for footpads, but apart from the odd peasant working the land he encountered no-one.

At length he breasted a rise in the ground and found himself looking down on the busy concourse of the Bridgewater canal, just as had Sam and his brother back in the spring, albeit much further back towards Manchester.

Cautiously he steered his mount down onto the towpath and hailed the crew of a passing barge.

'Which way and how far for Preston Brook, friends?'

The man leading the horse answered, 'Tis but no more than a mile or so, the same way we're heading, sir.'

Now that his quest might be coming to a conclusion, Regan was mulling over how best to go about actually making contact.

Of course, he had no idea if the young couple were even here and concluded that he needed a base from which to conduct his enquiries.

A couple of miles back from the canal he'd passed close to an imposing mansion and, as the winter dusk began to close in, he thought it prudent to seek a night's accommodation from whatever member of the local gentry resided there. He turned his horse and rode back across the fields until he reached the neatly cobbled courtyard of the grand residence.

On closer inspection, Regan realised that the house was obviously the home of a man of considerable wealth. The walls were of red brick, three stories high, and windows too numerous to count at first glance. From the condition of the brickwork, it seemed it was of fairly recent construction. Regan was a little apprehensive as to the welcome he might receive.

His approach had been observed. As he reached the massive front door it opened, and two boisterous lurchers bounded towards him, startling the horse. Fortunately, their welcome was a friendly one, as was the one of the portly gentleman who stood framed in the doorway.

'Good afternoon to you sir,' the man said. 'Can I be of assistance to you?'

'Good afternoon,' replied Regan. 'I have just ridden from Warrington, and wonder if I might beg a night's accommodation?'

'You are most welcome sir, to share our humble abode, here at Danthorp. It's not often that we are blessed with company, and I would be failing in my duty as an English gentleman to deny you a good dinner and a warm bed for the night.'

Regan thanked him gratefully, for although his journey from Warrington had been trouble free, he was beginning to feel a chill in his bones after his long ride.

'Come into the drawing room, my good sir, and warm yourself. Let me offer you a glass of madeira. I'll summon a groom to take care of your horse.'

Handing over his horse to the stable lad who had appeared promptly, Regan gratefully followed his host into a large hall.

The man ushered him through one of several doors into a spacious high-ceilinged room, tastefully decorated with duck egg blue walls. Large prints of country scenes and framed portraits hung from every wall. The grand furniture - elegant sofas, armchairs, and small tables - sat atop thick luxuriant rugs. It was obviously the home of not only a wealthy man, but one of exquisite taste.

It reminded him very much of his own home. It seemed a lifetime ago since he'd left Dunslaney, and a sudden surge of homesickness swept over Regan. The trappings of his own house had never meant much to him. He made a promise to himself that when he finally returned to Wexford, it would be with a new appreciation of his home. If the Fates were kind to him there would also be a young wife and a brother to share it with him. Despite her impoverished upbringing, Regan had no doubt that he could turn Mary into a fine lady to adorn Dunslaney.

'Take off your coat and boots my good fellow, and make yourself at home,' said the man. 'We live a fairly quiet life in these parts, it's always nice to welcome some company.'

'I thank you kindly for your friendly welcome,' replied Regan. 'It really is very good of you to offer your home to a total stranger.'

'The pleasure is all mine,' said the genial host. 'Have you business to conduct in this area, or is that too presumptuous a query?'

'Not at all,' replied Regan. 'I do indeed have an urgent matter to attend to and I must find my way to Preston Brook and the canal in the morning.'

'Ah, the famous Bridgewater canal,' exclaimed his host. 'It has certainly started a mighty series of undertakings, the like of which is unprecedented. So vast are the Duke's profits that suddenly the whole country is clamouring to build more and more waterways across the entire land. Do you have a financial interest in it, sir?'

'Oh no, nothing of that sort - my business is a strictly personal thing,' said Regan

'Please don't think me rude in my inquisitiveness,' the man went on. 'It's just that I have a considerable amount of capital tied up in this new canal, the Grand Junction, and I just wondered if you were similarly involved?'

'No sir,' continued Regan, 'I have journeyed across the sea from Wexford in order to find a pair of young people to whom a great injustice was done and to put matters right. I have reason to believe that they may be working on this new canal and hope to confirm my convictions tomorrow.'

'In that case, sir, I wish you well in your quest. I shall have a room prepared for you and invite you to share dinner with my wife and myself.'

'You really are a most generous man, sir,' said Regan. 'I think it's time to be formally introduced. My name is Fintan Regan of Dunslaney in County Wexford.'

He offered his hand to his host, who shook it enthusiastically.

'A pleasure to meet you sir. My name is Godfrey Crane, and my wife, Eliza, will hopefully join us directly.'

As if on cue the door opened and in swept an elegant lady in a low-cut gown of midnight blue.

Regan was immediately stuck by the obvious disparity between the ages of Mr. Crane and his beautiful young wife.

Her lustrous auburn hair was tightly curled above her head. An almost perfectly oval face and dark brown eyes all combined to make Regan catch his breath in awe. A surge of the old lust rushed to his loins at the sight of this vision of loveliness, which he hastily blocked from his mind.

'Godfrey,' said the lady, in a silvery tone which matched her demeanour perfectly. 'Lewis informed me that we have a guest. It is a pleasure to meet you sir. I trust my husband has been looking after you?'

She sat beside him on the roomy sofa and shook his hand.

Regan shivered involuntarily at the touch of her elegantly manicured fingers and answered, 'Oh yes indeed ma-am. I'm overwhelmed by your kindness to a total stranger.'

'It is a pleasure to be of service to you, we have so few guests especially this late in the year,' said the lady.

Crane made the introduction and informed his wife of Regan's mission.

'Oh, how charming,' enthused Eliza. 'To think you have made this epic journey for such a worthwhile cause, is truly admirable. I wish you every success.'

'It may prove a fruitless endeavour, but I must carry it through now I've come this far,' said Regan.

'There are many labourers from far and wide employed on this massive project, including a good number of your countrymen,' observed Crane. 'So, there is a good chance of success.'

'We hear a lot of stories and rumours from the work-ings,' chimed in Mrs Crane. 'Some weeks ago, we heard that a young apprentice was killed when a horse kicked him in the head. Such a tragedy, but that is the nature of the job. I fear that many more will be maimed or worse before it is completed.'

They continued to make conversation for some time until a manservant appeared and informed them that a guest chamber had been made ready and a hip bath was waiting for Regan.

The servant led him to the room and said deferentially, 'If sir would like to leave his under garments, they will be washed and aired ready for the morning. Mr Crane has instructed me to find you some suitable apparel for this evening. Dinner will be served at eight.'

Regan was once again astonished by the level of the generosity of this wonderful household and vowed to leave a handsome tip in the morning. He couldn't help feeling perplexed as to how such a beautiful young creature as Eliza could possibly be married to a man of such portliness, obviously old enough to be her father.

He resolved to keep these thoughts very much to himself. Perhaps all would become clear as the night wore on.

He joined the Cranes for dinner, in a small impeccably furnished dining room. An oval walnut table with matching chairs and sideboards added to the opulence.

Eliza had changed into another beautiful gown of russet coloured silk, which seemed to enhance her astonishing beauty all the more.

Once again Regan struggled to avoid staring in open-mouthed admiration and tried to concentrate on what his host was saying.

Crane was waxing enthusiastically on the subject of the canal mania that was sweeping the country. It seemed that every month a new Act of Parliament was being passed to enable yet another waterway to be started - the aim being to link all parts of the nation and thus bring great prosperity.

Regan had heard of a similar undertaking in Ireland to link Dublin with the Shannon but had paid it scant regard. He made a mental note to find out more about the venture when he returned.

Crane had offered to accompany him to the worksite on the morrow, saying, 'If you'll allow me, I'll go with you in the morning. I often call on Davies the manager there, and I'd be glad to introduce you.'

'That is a very good idea sir,' replied Regan. 'It would indeed be very helpful.'

After a fine meal, Eliza retired to her room and the two men spent a couple of hours with brandy and cigars in affable conversation.

When Regan eventually returned to his comfortable room, he thanked the heavens for leading him to this admirable place. He was no nearer solving the conundrum of his mismatched hosts' marital arrangement, but after his long day he was soon in a deep untroubled sleep.

Chapter Twenty-Four

The morning of the first day of December was a chilly, foggy affair and the various gangs of workmen made their way back to the tunnel with little to cheer them, apart from the prospect of the promised bonus that would soon be theirs.

It could only be a matter of days before the tunnellers at the shaft broke through to the gang working inwards from the north portal. Similarly, other gangs were working from the south portal northwards. The obvious goal was to have the whole undertaking completed before the year's end.

Medlock's men were engaged in the shaft and faced the prospect of yet another gruelling day in the gloomy wet conditions. Sam's only consolation was to know that he'd be returning each night to the arms of his nubile young wife.

Each night it seemed that their mutual ardour was forging an ever-stronger bond between them, and it was the thought of her love that kept him sane as he hacked away at the never-ending wall of rock and mud before him.

Back at the compound the women were busy with their usual tasks of clearing and tidying the canteen area and preparing the day's food for the workforce. Tess was becoming used to the gentle, bawdy teasing on her newly-wed status. It was a gleeful company of ladies laughing and joking their way through the morning. Little did they know how the situation was to change in so short a time.

* * *

Regan and Crane had enjoyed a hearty substantial breakfast and at ten o'clock set out on the ride of three miles or so to the canal junction.

They picked their way cautiously through the thick December fog and arrived at the compound at a little after eleven.

They dismounted and approached the office where they encountered Davies poring over his account books.

'Ah, Mr Crane,' he said, as he stood up. 'Always a pleasure to see you sir, and with company I see!'

'Good morning, Mr. Davies,' replied Crane. 'My companion is Mr Regan from the county of Wexford in Ireland.'

Regan and Davies shook hands, and Regan wasted no time in stating the reason for his call.

'I hope you may be able to help me in a certain matter, sir,' he addressed Davies. 'I have journeyed many weeks and hundreds of miles in search of a pair of young Irish people - a lad and a lass who I have reason to believe might be here working for you.'

Davies, immediately on his guard, enquired cautiously, 'And what might be the reason for your mission, sir?'

'It is a personal thing between myself and the pair of which I speak, but I can assure you I mean them no harm,' replied Regan.

'As I'm sure you will be aware, sir,' countered Davies, 'many people from far and wide come here seeking work, including a good proportion of your countrymen. I don't recall such a pair. A lad and a girl, did you say? Have you any idea of when they would have arrived here?'

'It was probably in August or early September I'd say from information I already possess,' said Regan.

'I will check my register.' Davies made a great show of opening and scanning a huge ledger book on his desk. He had no intention of complying with this stranger's request - not at first anyway. He felt he needed more knowledge of the man's motives before divulging any details. He guessed instinctively that young Will and Teresa were the couple that Regan was seeking, but he certainly wasn't about to reveal that fact.

'No sir, I'm sorry there is no record of a young couple arriving together. Besides which, 'tis mostly men and boys that seek work here, not young lasses.'

'May I see that ledger for myself?' asked Regan respectfully.

'I'm sorry, that will not be possible,' was Davies' wary reply.

'In that case,' Regan asked, with a note of exasperation in his voice, 'will you escort me to where the men are working, to see if anybody has heard of the couple I seek?'

'That too, will not be practicable, good sir. Most of them are working in the tunnel and will not return until nightfall. I'm very sorry, but I don't think I can be of further assistance to you, so I bid you good day gentlemen.'

With that Davies ushered the visitors outside and shut the door firmly on them.

'Well, that would appear to be that,' sighed Crane. 'It seems your long journey has proved to be in vain. It's such a pity after all that you've endeavoured to achieve.'

'I'm not so sure, Godfrey,' answered Regan. 'Did you not note the prevarication in that man's manner? Most evasive and unhelpful, which leads me to believe that he's covering something up.'

'That's as may be Fintan, but I've always found him very honest and informative,' answered Crane. 'Perhaps your suspicions are unfounded. Let us return to Danthorp and ponder the matter further.'

Reluctantly, Regan agreed and they remounted for the return journey.

The fog had cleared somewhat and as they left the yard, they encountered a group of six or seven women hanging laundry on a washing line. Regan swiftly inspected them from his horse. They seemed to be of varying ages and appearance. He held his mount still and stared at the group but could see no sign of a young girl with long brown hair, and so rode off in frustration after Crane.

Teresa, however, had seen the pair of riders depart, and shivered in dread, for although her view of them was from a distance, there seemed something familiar about the upright stance in the saddle of one of them, and she sank to her knees in despair.

The other women gathered round her in consternation, helping her back to her feet.

'Jesus, girl,' gasped Annie. 'Whatever ails thee? Looks like you've seen a ghost.'

Teresa was completely tongue-tied with shock and was helped to a bench outside the storehouse.

Davies, seeing the distress of the young bride was left in no doubt as to the cause. He was much relieved that his caution had put Regan off the scent. He was in little doubt, however, that Regan would return with more questioning.

He brought Teresa into his office and, sensing that she needed privacy and calm, told the other women to leave her alone for a while.

After the women had left, he bade Teresa to sit on the stool facing his desk.

'Now, my dear,' he said gently. 'It's obvious to me that the stranger who just left has brought on your state of shock. If you'd like to tell me more, I'm willing to listen. I'll send someone to bring your husband back, and if you prefer to wait until he attends you, I will understand.'

He went to a cabinet and produced a bottle of brandy.

'Here, Tess, take a sip of this to calm you.'

Teresa felt the fiery liquid coursing through her veins, warming and soothing her tremors of fear.

'Was one of those men named Regan?' she stuttered brokenly.

'Ay, that's what he said,' replied Davies. 'I presume that you and poor young Will are the people he's come after - all the way from Ireland. He said he means you no harm.'

'Oh merciful Jesus, so it was him. Did you tell him I was here?'

'Oh no, lass. Credit me with more sense than that,' said Davies, somewhat querulously. 'But if you want me to help you, it would be advisable to tell me why the tracing of a young lass is important enough to bring him all this way.'

'I will tell you sir,' sobbed Teresa, 'but let me wait until my husband returns.'

'Of course, lass. Just sit quietly until Sam gets here. Here, have a little more brandy to soothe ye.'

Half an hour later, a mud-stained Sam arrived accompanied by George Medlock. He rushed anxiously to his panic-stricken wife.

'I think it's time we all put matters straight, don't you?' said Davies. 'Honesty is always the best way forward.'

'Sam, an Irish gentleman came here this morning in the company of one of our major shareholders and enquired after a young Irish couple. I immediately realised that it was Teresa and Will he was searching for, but I sent him away with no information. I fear he was not satisfied with my denial and will probably return, so if I am to be of assistance to you, I need to know what it is that he seeks.'

'Let me speak for you my lovely girl,' said Sam to his bewildered and terrified wife.

'I'll tell you what I know,' he continued to Davies and Medlock.

'Teresa and Will surely are the couple he's after,' said Sam solemnly. 'He was their master and he treated them with great cruelty and abuse. They stole some money and a watch and made their escape on his favourite horse. They rode all the way to Dublin and stowed away on a ship bound for Liverpool. After almost being captured twice they made it to Warrington and then to here.'

'I am naught but a common thief,' sobbed Teresa. 'If he takes me back, I'll surely hang.'

'Shush, lass,' said Davies soothingly. 'He has to find you first. I have no intention of letting that happen. I can't begin to imagine the courage and resolve you have shown to get here. Whatever you did in the past is of no concern to me. Of course, poor Will has already paid a terrible price.'

'I'll say one thing more though,' he added. 'The manner of his enquiry seemed to suggest that he wanted to make amends rather than seek vengeance.'

'He's a cruel monster,' cried Teresa. 'I know exactly what he'll do with me if he finds me.'

'Well, we'll have to make sure that doesn't happen,' said Davies firmly.

Turning to Sam he continued, 'I think that the best thing would be if you took some time off and visited your family with your new bride.'

'But what about my work here?' asked Sam anxiously.

'Don't concern thysen with that, lad,' put in Medlock. 'There'll allus be a job here for thee, I'll see to that.'

'Right, that's settled then,' said Davies. 'No need for you to travel by horse now. There are passenger boats as well as coal barges now, so we'll get you the morning one - the day after tomorrow. So, prepare yourselves for the journey and keep your wits about you for the time being, just in case he returns.'

Sam shook Davies' hand and thanked him warmly for saving the situation. Arms around his still traumatised wife he led her to their hut to discuss the calamity that had beset them, and to prepare for their flight from the area.

Teresa still had over ten pounds left and together with the twelve pounds or so that Sam had earned and left with Davies, they had ample funds for the journey and for Sam's family reunion. Although it was still only a little after noon, Sam had no intention of returning to his work.

Thoughtfully, Davies left them to it. They retired to their hut. Sam tried everything to calm the frightened lass, with little success.

'Oh, Sam,' she sighed, 'I just knew he'd never give up. He won't be satisfied until he puts a noose around my neck.'

'Try not to vex yourself, my love,' said Sam.

He held her close and went on, 'We'll be away soon enough, and I know Mr. Davies and George will never tell him where we've gone.'

After the evening meal, they retired early, too distracted by the day's events to even think of making love. Fearful of what the new day had in store they eventually fell asleep in each other's arms.

Chapter Twenty-Five

Regan rode back with Crane to Danthorp in a mood of black despair. He was convinced that he was on the right track - there were too many coincidences for it not to be true. There was something nagging at his brain telling him that he had missed a vital clue at the compound.

They arrived to the disconcerting news that, in their absence, Eliza had tripped on the staircase and sprained her ankle. The surgeon Towers from Preston on the Hill was in attendance.

'Tis not serious sir,' he advised Crane. 'I have bound it and given laudanum and brandy for the pain. She should rest for a week or so by which time, hopefully, it will have healed.'

'Thank you, Mr Towers, for your swift attendance,' said a relieved Crane. 'As the night is drawing in, won't you please stay for the night and take dinner with us.'

'That is an excellent suggestion sir. I thank you kindly. The journey home is quite hazardous in the dark.'

The three men retired to Crane's study, where the usual fine sherry was served, and introductions made.

They made small talk for a while and then Regan informed Towers of the reason for his visit and his lack of success.

'Did you say 'twas a young lad and a lass that you seek, sir?' asked Towers.

'It is so, but Davies says no such people have been engaged, so it seems I have made a long journey for no reward,' answered Regan ruefully.

'That is most odd,' remarked Towers. 'Back in the summer - mid July if my memory serves me - I was called to the compound to attend a young lad who'd been kicked in the head by a colt he was trying to shoe. To make matters worse he'd fallen back against an anvil and suffered further head wounds. He had gone into a coma. I did all I could for the boy but sadly he never recovered and died three days later.'

'Good God, man,' gasped Regan. 'I knew it. Davies was lying all along. Did they tell you his name?'

'They said it was Will. The women attending him all seemed to be Irish by their tongue, so I presumed that the unfortunate boy was too.'

'Oh yes, I'm on the right track surely. Was there a young girl among them?'

'There was indeed a pretty waif who sat by him holding his hand and crying pitifully.'

'Had she long brown hair?'

'Her hair was certainly brown but cut very short almost like a lad.'

Regan paced the room triumphantly.

'I saw her, Godfrey!' he gushed fervently. 'D'ye mind those washer women we saw. I'm convinced she was one of them!'

'It certainly seems that Davies was covering for them,' remarked Crane, adding, 'actually, just the girl, as the poor lad is no longer with us.'

The news suddenly hit Regan hard. One of his two objectives was no longer attainable. His half-brother young Joe Molloy would never inherit the fortune waiting at home for him.

'Did the lad have a Christian burial?' asked Regan choking on his emotion.

'He was buried in a pauper's grave in Preston church-yard,' answered Towers. 'Like so many of the itinerants who come here for work, no-one knows who they are or whether there are families to be informed. So, the parish does it's best for them. I can show you the spot if you wish, sir.'

'That would be very good of you, Mr Towers. I may as well tell ye both now. The lad's real name was Joseph, and he was my half-brother. I never knew that fact until he'd fled. I had always been led to believe that he was just a lowly stable hand. As for the girl, Mary, that's another story. Suffice to say I must find her and bring her home.'

'Well, well,' remarked Crane. 'It seems we must return on the morrow. I have considerable holdings in the Company and will certainly bring pressure to bear upon Davies. If he values his position, he'd better be more forthcoming.'

Despite taking a soothing hot bath and donning the clothes that Crane had loaned him, Regan was so tautly wound up, he just couldn't relax.

He picked moodily through the excellent mutton that he'd been served, unable to do it justice. However, he drank glass after glass of his host's French wine.

'Go easy, Fintan!' warned Crane. 'You'll need your wits about you in the morning.'

'Dammit, Godfrey, you're right of course,' replied Regan. 'It's just the thought that I was within touching distance of that beloved girl after all these weeks.'

'Does she mean so much to you, then?' asked Crane.

'I can't tell you all of it, my friend. To my eternal shame, I have wronged her badly, and will not rest until I hold her in my arms or grovel at her feet. I'll bid you goodnight, for who knows what tomorrow holds in store for me.'

He retired once more to the bedroom, where despite the copious amount of wine he'd consumed, he spent a restless night.

The news of young Joe's tragic end was hard for him to bear. He remembered, with shame, all the times he'd chastised him. His former arrogant way with all his underlings was something he'd regret for the rest of his days. He looked forward to the morning and the chance to be reunited with the dear creature who'd brought such a profound change to his ways.

Chapter Twenty-Six

Another morning of dense chilling fog did nothing to lift Teresa's spirits. She was convinced that Regan somehow would not only find her, but also bring constables to place her under arrest and force her to go back to Wexford.

Although Sam did all he could to boost her morale, deep down he was also fearful for the future. The promised passage on the canal could not happen until the following day - the passenger carriage service was limited to a twice weekly occurrence at present - and so they were going to have to keep a very low profile for the next twenty-four hours.

What if Regan could summon sufficient authority to organise a thorough search of the compound. Sam, just a poor farm boy at heart, had no knowledge of how such an eventuality might be possible, but feared that the rich could do pretty much as they pleased. The law would always be weighted in their favour. The only possible solution to his mind was for them to hide themselves in the surrounding woods - a grim prospect at this time of year.

He expressed his anxiety to Medlock over breakfast and together with Davies they pondered over how to conceal

Tess from Regan's search party, if indeed it came to that eventuality. After much pondering Medlock had a sudden flash of inspiration which he shared with his young protégé.

'It sounds a bit daft,' said Medlock. 'But it might just work. Tell thy missus to don every bit of warm clothing she has and the pair of ye come with me. We'll hide her int' tunnel. The buggers won't come looking for her there!'

So Tess, dressed in Sam's spare breeches and smock and a massive greatcoat belonging to Medlock, joined her husband and the other members of Medlock's gang trudging their way to the tunnel.

They arrived and went to the shaft at the top. Sam descended by using the metal rungs in the brickwork. Then it was Teresa's turn. She shook with trepidation as she climbed into the bucket. She clung desperately to the rim as it swayed from side to side in its descent into the black pit. For a few terrifying moments she was back in the hold of the Foxhunter, but after what seemed an age, but in reality was no more than three minutes, the bucket hit the ground with a jolt.

Sam helped her out and they held each other in a close embrace as the bucket was hauled back up and then lowered again with Tom Docherty and a new man, Brian Ashby who'd been taken on a couple of weeks previously, as its passengers.

Teresa stumbled along the muddy floor of the cavern, following closely behind Sam, who was stopping every few yards to light candles.

To the young bride, it seemed unbelievably cold in that dark hole. She could only sit on a huge rock, that Sam hewed out for her, and watch as Sam and Tom picked at the rock and soil. Matt and the new man loaded the spoil into a barrow and took it back to the bucket.

All morning poor Teresa tried to keep out of the way as the men worked. Despite the winter coat she was soon blue with cold. Sam did his best to keep her warm by stopping every few minutes to hug her to him. At long last Medlock sent word that it was safe to return to the compound.

* * *

Regan and Crane had indeed arrived an hour or so after Teresa had been spirited away but, after a long parley with Davies, they'd left again.

There had been a long and crucial two-hour conflict at the office.

On arrival they had immediately confronted the manager.

'Mr Davies,' began Crane, gravely. 'You will know that I have a considerable holding in the Company which employs you, and that a word in the right ear could have serious implications for your position here. This gentleman and I have discovered irrefutable evidence that the fugitives he seeks did come here.'

'I'm sorry, sir,' replied Davies, defiantly. 'I repeat I have no knowledge of them.'

'That's a damnable lie!' roared Regan. 'The body of Joseph Molloy, or Will as he was known here, lies in a pauper's grave no more than a mile hence. I have seen it with my own eyes. He was my own brother damn you, and my heart is broken.'

Seizing the startled Davies by the lapels of his jacket he continued, 'I will have the truth, you blaggard, or not only will you lose your job here, but I shall have you arrested.'

A crestfallen Davies, realising that the time for subterfuge was over, decided that he had no option but to change his story to one he'd worked out with Medlock and Sam when they'd had the crazy notion of hiding the girl in the tunnel.

'All right, gentlemen,' he began, his voice trembling with consternation. 'I'll confess that I have concealed the truth, but hear me out. I did so because the young girl is terrified of you, Mr Regan. She has seen much hardship and tragedy in her young life, and I felt honour bound to assist her.'

'She has nothing to fear from me,' murmured Regan in a much softer tone. 'I have come all this way to atone for my mistreatment of both of them. It's too late for poor Joe, but Mary, for that is her real name, means the world to me. I have come to take her home and make her my wife.'

Davies sighed and shook his head, 'You'd better take a seat sir,' he said. For I have news for you that you will be greatly disappointed to hear.'

'Go on, man. Out with it!' replied Regan.

'Mary, or Teresa as she now wishes to be known, is a married woman now.'

'Whaaat!' exclaimed Regan. 'No I don't believe it - I won't believe it.'

'Nonetheless it's true. I witnessed the ceremony myself, along with several other people here, who can attest that it is so. Let God be my judge. She was married a mere two weeks or so past to a young English lad who was working here.'

Regan, head in hands, gave a groan of despair.

'Oh God, say it's not true. I've lost them both, and all I wanted was to make things whole between us.'

Facing Davies again, he continued, 'Take me to her, I need to see her. She has to know that I have made it my only desire to right past wrongs.'

'Sadly, sir,' said Davies. 'That, too, will not be possible. It seems she saw you yesterday, and the sight of you filled her with such dread that she and husband have taken flight.'

Regan thumped the desk in anguish.

'Sweet Jesus, what am I to do now,' he wailed disconsolately,

'I still don't trust a word you say Davies. I'm damned if I'll leave here until I have solid proof of their departure.'

'I can assure you that it's true,' answered Davies.

Opening a ledger on the desk, he bade Regan and Crane to examine it.

'As you can see, this is the wages book, and the latest entry is dated yesterday. Sam Burton, her husband, came to me and appraised me of the situation. He said he needed what was owed to him, for he had to take his wife away to stop her falling into your clutches. I paid him the twelve pounds that had accrued He was so desperate and determined to leave, he even forfeited the three-guinea bonus that was to become due to him when the tunnel is completed.'

Regan and Crane were completely dumbfounded by this revelation.

'I can show you their living quarters, if you wish,' continued Davies 'Although you'll find nothing there. Everything they owned has gone. They left at first light - it seems evident that they have no intention of returning.'

'Well which way did they go?' asked Crane. 'Were they on foot?'

'They went south on horseback,' answered Davies. 'They were last seen going over the top of the new tunnel.' He glanced at his pocket watch. 'It was at least three hours since.'

'Did they steal a horse, then?' asked Regan. 'Or did you give them one?'

Davies hadn't allowed for that perceptive observation and had to think rapidly.

'No, they didn't steal it,' he said, swallowing hard. 'It was an old mare, past its prime. I let Sam have it in lieu of the bonus he was not going to get.'

'Where was this Sam from originally?' asked Crane.

Davies was getting very hot under the collar at the persistence of this questioning but struggled manfully on despite the feeling that he was getting himself in ever deeper water.

'I never knew that. I seem to remember he'd mentioned that his father was a tenant of the Duke, so it was probably somewhere near Manchester.'

'Yet they set off south in a direction that he knew nothing of,' mused Crane. 'The easier option would have been to return to his home.'

'I can only surmise that he thought he'd find work further down the cut - I understand there are new side branches under construction in the Staffordshire area,' said Davies. 'I'm afraid he didn't take me into his confidence - they just took off so quickly.'

'Show me just the route they took" demanded Regan.

'But of course,' replied a relieved Davies, hoping for a swift end of the matter.

He led them along the towpath as far as the tunnel and took them to the top of the hill, to where the five shafts were visible at intervals of a few hundred yards.

'That's the way they must have gone,' said Davies. 'This is where the Grand Junction starts all the way down to the Trent in Derbyshire.'

Regan sat astride his mount and peered through the gloom of the short winter day as if willing Mary to appear before him. He sat in silence for a few minutes and then without a word to his companions turned his horse and made his way back to the tunnel entrance. He had no way of knowing that moments before, whilst he was at the top of the hill, the object of his mission was shivering in a hole some twenty yards beneath his feet.

Chapter Twenty-Seven

Teresa was hauled from the depths of the tunnel almost rigid with cold.

'Best ye get her back into the warm as quick as you can, lad,' said Medlock to Sam.

Sam needed no second bidding and as they made their way back, they met the other women leading a horse and cart loaded with the steaming cauldrons of the midday broth.

Teresa gratefully thanked Lizzie for the beaker of the hot food that she was handed. She sipped the nourishing brew, it's warmth going some way to revive her, and they continued back to the warmth of the kitchen area.

Davies welcomed the young couple.

'Twas a close call, but I hope and pray we've seen the last of Mr. Regan. I told him that you'd gone south over the tunnel. I think we've done enough to convince him.'

'We can't thank you enough sir,' said Sam. 'My poor girl lives in mortal terror of that monster.'

'I have to say, Sam,' remarked Davies, 'once he got over his rage at being deceived, he said all he wanted to do was make amends.'

Addressing Teresa, he continued, 'He told me that young Will's real name was Joseph Molloy. Did you know that?'

'Yes, sir I did,' answered Teresa. 'We changed our names to cover our tracks, but I fear it didn't work.'

'Did you also know that poor Will or Joseph was Mr. Regan's brother?'

Teresa visibly paled and gasped, 'No, I didn't know that and nor did Will. He would surely have told me if it was so. It's probably another of Regan's lies to make me feel sorry for him.'

'Well, I suppose we'll never know the truth of that,' continued Davies. 'But let's get the pair of you away tomorrow. I fear he may not be done with us yet.'

* * *

On that grey winter afternoon, a bitterly disappointed Regan accompanied Crane back to the welcoming warmth of Danthorp Hall.

'Come, Fintan. Let us take a madeira or two and contemplate the day's events,' said Crane.

'I really can't take it all in,' said Regan. 'I'm convinced that Davies was keeping something from us. Something about the speed in which they took flight just doesn't ring true.'

'Even if that is so,' countered Crane, 'there is naught you can do to alter the fact that the object of your desires is now married to another man.'

Regan's shoulders slumped in despair. 'To think I've travelled so far and gone to such lengths on a wild goose chase.'

'Ay, it's a bitter blow for you,' said Crane sympathetically. 'Take comfort in knowing that you've done your level best to right past wrongs - let your conscience be at peace.'

'I suppose you're right,' sighed Regan. 'I really can't impose on your hospitality any longer. On the morrow I shall return to Warrington and my boy and prepare for home.'

'You have a son?' asked Crane in astonishment.

'Yes, my son's name is Henry. He's fourteen and I left him in the capable hands of my secretary Edward Dunn at the Red Lion in Warrington.'

'Ah, well. At least you have the love of a child for solace. Not a joy that will ever be known to Eliza and I unfortunately,' said Crane, ruefully. 'My wife cannot give me a child.'

'I'm sorry to hear that,' said Regan. 'Such kind generous bodies as yourselves should not be denied the gift of progeny.'

'Alas, that is the way of it,' said Crane. 'Although we're blessed in other ways. I have a considerable income from my business interests. I purchased this property some years ago and transformed it from a state of dereliction to what you see now.'

'Most impressive!' remarked Regan. 'Do you think that this present propensity towards canal building is going to last, or is it just a flash in the pan?'

'Good Lord, no man!' exclaimed Crane. 'Canals will be the making of this country. Just look at Francis Egerton, the Duke of Bridgewater. He almost bankrupted himself in the building of his canal and now he's making vast profits from the hauling of coal to Manchester and Liverpool.'

He went on, 'People are falling over themselves to invest in a great network that will link all the major ports to one another - even as far south as the capital itself. If I were you sir, I'd think very carefully of at least dipping your toe in the water, so to speak.'

Crane's enthusiasm was becoming quite convincing, and Regan's mind was already filling with thoughts of what might be achievable back in Ireland. After a couple of hours of this stimulating talk and several glasses of the excellent sherry, the bitter sense of failure at the outcome of his futile quest was gradually fading.

Later, over dinner, the bond of friendship and mutual respect between the Cranes and Regan took even firmer hold.

'It has been an enlightening experience for me to be here,' said Regan. He was becoming more and more charmed by the stunning beauty of his hostess and was at great pains not to let that admiration become too obvious.

He went on, 'I have never left my homeland before. It has certainly been a journey of contrasts. My quest has ended in bitter failure, but I feel I have found two delightful new friends.'

'That feeling is mutual,' replied Eliza. 'I'm so sorry, Fintan, that things haven't turned out as you had hoped. You must console yourself with the thought that you did your utmost to make amends.'

'Hear, hear!' added Crane. 'Let us agree to exchange correspondence from time to time, and perhaps one day we might contemplate a visit to your home.'

'That is an excellent idea!' said Regan. 'You would both be made very welcome.'

After a convivial evening and a nightcap of brandy and a cigar, Regan retired to his chamber to reflect on his failed quest. Through dogged determination and a little good fortune, he had tracked the runaways down, but the outcome had been a bitter disappointment.

He'd relished the thought of telling Joseph of his true identity, only to find that the poor lad was gone from the world, never to know of his inheritance. His feelings for Mary were confusing to him. He realised that he'd been chasing an impossible dream. His hopes were now shattered beyond all repair, and yet… the nagging feeling persisted that Davies was covering something up.

He hadn't produced any actual witnesses to the wedding, so that alone could be a falsehood. Their speedy flight also seemed just too convenient to be true. He could understand Mary's fear of him and yearned for a few moments alone with her to convince her of his sincerity. He'd beg her to return with him and, despite her lowly station, vow to make her a lady. He eventually drifted off, determined to visit the canal compound and confront Davies one last time.

Chapter Twenty-Eight

The following morning dawned crisp and clear after a hard frost.

Regan took an early last breakfast with his hosts and prepared for his departure. Eliza and Godfrey went into the courtyard to see him off. Regan told them of his continuing uncertainty and stated that he intended to make one last effort to get to the bottom of the mystery.

'Godfrey, I have spent a restless night turning yesterday's events over and over in my mind. I swear that Davies is lying and that the whole charade is just a cover up to throw me off the scent.'

'Fintan, my dear friend,' replied Crane. 'I beg you, for your own good to forget this obsession. You'll drive yourself to madness by it. Return to Wexford - enjoy watching your boy mature. There are plenty of women, I'll be bound, only to eager to bring you contentment.'

Regan dismissed this sound advice, 'I'll have no peace until I've made one last attempt to discover the truth. Davies' story is just too damned convenient. Even the so-called marriage may be a sham.'

'Well, if you won't take my advice, so be it,' replied Crane, 'I can see no point in my travelling with you but be assured there will always be a welcome for you here at Danthorp.'

'Godfrey, I will be eternally grateful for the kindness and assistance you have given so freely, but I'm determined on the path I must take. I have to know. If my final attempt proves in vain, then I will surely do as you advise.'

He mounted his horse and reached down to shake Godfrey's hand.

'Of one thing I'm certain. I have made noble friends in you sir, and your good lady. I bid you farewell in the hope that should you ever wish to see my country, it would be an honour to return your wonderful hospitality.'

With that Regan set off for the canal for the last time.

The route from Danthorp to the canal was over open country. As he approached, Regan pondered on how to conceal his presence for as long as possible. On the previous times he'd ridden this route, he'd noticed a small thicket of trees on a rise overlooking the compound. He approached with caution, dismounted and tethered the horse to a thick overhanging branch. Back in Warrington among his purchases, he'd obtained a spyglass. He put it to use now to excellent effect. He had a clear view of the area outside the office and storehouse.

* * *

The passenger boat for Manchester was to leave at 9.30am from the junction. Sam estimated that it would take five hours or so to reach Barton, where he and Teresa would have just enough daylight left to complete the rest of the journey on foot, as he had in what seemed a lifetime ago.

A small party, including Annie and some of the other women, had gathered to see them off.

Davies shook Sam firmly by the hand and wished him well, saying, 'Now Sam, by the grace of God, this tunnel will be completed before the year's end. If you return seeking more work, you may well find that we're no longer here. However, as George here will confirm, we shall be seeking to form our own little company to bid for work further south at a place called Caldon, and you, my lad, will always find employment with us, so think on.'

'Ay, indeed, Sam,' said Medlock. 'I hate to see ye go, but ye just look after that sweet lass of thine and Godspeed the pair of ye.'

* * *

Regan scanned the scene from his hiding place and a surge of triumph coursed through his veins, for there in plain sight stood the object of his desires in the midst of a small gathering of people. It had been her much shorter hair and male apparel that had prevented him from identifying her on his first visit.

Just as he'd thought, yesterday's pretence was a tissue of lies from the outset. From the embracing and hand shaking he observed taking place, it was clear there wasn't a moment to lose.

Rapt in making their fond farewells, none of those present noticed the lone figure approaching the compound. He dodged between the buildings and piles of bricks until he was close by. Before anybody could stop him, he rushed at Teresa from behind and pinioning her arms held the terrified girl in front of him.

CHAPTER TWENTY-EIGHT

'I knew all along that you, Davies, had told me a string of lies,' he roared.

Still holding the screaming wretched Teresa by one arm he withdrew his short sword and brandished it at the company in general.

'Stay back, all of you. Keep well away.'

He murmured to the distraught girl, 'Mary, my dearest treasure. I've travelled all this way, not to punish you, but to make amends for the way I abused you so. I want to take you home and make you mistress of Dunslaney.'

'For God's sake let her go,' shouted Sam despairingly 'She's not going anywhere with you, you filthy scoundrel. She's my wife.'

Still brandishing the sword Regan replied, 'From what I've seen here, I doubt that you're legally wed at all. Mary, I beg you, leave this peasant boy behind and come home with me and be my lady. I swear I'll never mistreat you again. I'm a much-changed man.'

'Now stand aside, all of you,' he commanded menacingly. 'She's a simple Irish lass who belongs in her native land with a native Irishman.'

'No, no I hate you!' the girl shrieked. 'Let me go'.

She struggled and writhed but Regan had twisted her arm up behind her back, rendering her resistance futile.

It seemed a deadly impasse had been reached. No-one dare approach Regan for fear of him stabbing them or even worse his victim. Slowly he inched away from the company, dragging the helpless girl back towards the thicket.

There had been, however, one notable absentee from the farewell gathering.

Lizzie Mulryan had been at the well behind the store-house drawing a pail of water.

Hearing the angry shouts at the canal side, she concealed herself behind the building. Like everyone else, she'd been very aware that they probably hadn't seen the last of Mr. Regan and quickly surmised what was happening.

Stealing up behind the unsighted Regan and the writhing sobbing girl, she lifted the heavy pail and threw its contents all over them. Regan received the majority of the freezing cold water all over his head and shoulders and was so shocked that he released his grip on Teresa.

Lizzie, her blood well and truly up, swung the empty bucket and sent the sword spinning from his grasp.

Sam, seizing the opportunity that Lizzie's bold actions had presented to him, made a charge at Regan and wrestled him to the ground.

The two of them kicking and punching one another, turned over and over, and were soon at the water's edge.

The hard frost had made the towpath treacherously slippery. Such was the desperate nature of their struggle that the inevitable happened and they plunged into the icy water of the canal.

The bystanders, who had up to this point just stood by ineffectually watching the two protagonists, now swung into action.

It seemed obvious that both Sam and Regan, from their hopeless floundering in the water were unable to swim. Medlock seized a coiled rope from the side of the storehouse and lowered it into the canal. Sam clutched at it gratefully and was quickly hauled onto the quay.

Regan, however, was in a perilous state, trying despairingly to keep his head above the freezing murky depths.

Medlock shouted, 'Hold my legs,' as he prostrated himself over the edge. Two of the timber yard workers who'd also been present, did as they were bid and Medlock, straining every muscle in his body, managed to grasp the drowning man's forearm.

The same rope that had literally been Sam's lifeline was lowered again and after several vain attempts with Medlock's vice like grip beginning to weaken, Regan at last managed to take hold of it and slowly, inch by agonising inch, was dragged to the safety of the quay.

Sam, whose delivery from the water had been the quicker, was none the worse for his ordeal and was swiftly taken into the warmth of the dining area. A bath of welcome hot water was speedily prepared, and Sam stripped off his soaked muddy clothing and immersed himself. His visibly distressed young wife began to bathe him sobbing with a mixture of shock and relief as she did so.

'Don't worry, Tess,' he said. 'Your worst nightmare is well and truly over. Did they pull him out or let the swine drown?'

'Oh, Sam. If only it was true but no, Mr. Medlock managed to save him.'

Although he'd been pulled from the water, Regan lay shivering on the quayside - a pitiful looking half-drowned wretch.

'I suppose we'll have to get him inside,' said Davies. 'No point in dragging him out to let him freeze to death, though he deserves little sympathy.'

Another bath was made ready almost alongside Sam's.

Teresa visibly cringed with fear as a bedraggled Regan was helped to undress and get into the reviving hot water.

She almost vomited with revulsion at the memory of the very first time he'd assaulted her and robbed her of her virtue.

This, however, was a very different person to the swaggering master of Dunslaney. He sat shivering in the water, downcast and bewildered, teeth chattering, staring into the middle distance.

Sam asked Teresa to leave him alone with Regan and she needed no second bidding to make herself scarce. Incongruously, the two men sat in their adjacent baths in awkward silence.

Eventually Regan broke the ice. He cleared his throat and said in a hoarse whisper, 'Sam, if I may call you so, I have to speak my mind.'

'All right. I'm prepared to listen,' answered Sam dubiously.

'I don't know what Mary has told you,' began Regan.

'Don't call her Mary, she's Teresa now.'

'As you wish. No matter how it looks, I meant her no harm. It was a foolish impulse that made me act the way I did. The final desperate gesture of a defeated man.'

He continued, 'When she ran away from me, I realised how harshly I'd used her and I became full of contrition. I realise now that I have been engaged on a fool's errand. I should never embarked on such a hare-brained scheme.'

Sam could think of nothing to say so waited for the other man to continue.

For a few moments there was an awkward silence, before Regan went on, 'You have won her, Sam. I accept that she doesn't even want me to beg her forgiveness. I'll leave it to you to convey to her what I want to say, and I pledge on my son's life never to pursue her further.'

'That's all very well,' replied Sam. 'I'm grateful to you sir, for your openness. I know she wants to return the money she took when she fled.'

'Oh no!' exclaimed Regan. 'That was never the reason for my pursuit of her and Joe. I found out that he was my half-brother, and all I ever wanted was the chance to put things right and bring them both home.'

'I'm sorry to hear that, Mr Regan. Will seemed a fine lad and devoted to Teresa. I know she still misses him sorely.'

'It will be my lot in life to carry this burden of guilt to my death bed,' said Regan sadly. 'I never knew of his heritage until it was too late, and my abuse of him as a lowly servant drove him and Mary – sorry Teresa – to their flight for freedom, and ultimately to his tragic end.'

There seemed nothing more to add, and the two men continued sitting in silence until the rapid cooling of their bath water compelled them to seek to step out and dry themselves on the rough towelling that the women had provided.

Meanwhile at Danthorp, Crane and his wife had been discussing Regan's visit, his mission, and the manner of his departure.

'Godfrey,' said Eliza. 'I'm troubled by the thought of what may happen this morning at Preston Brook. What if Fintan's suspicions have a foundation and the girl is still there? I dread to think of what may happen.'

You're right, my dear,' agreed Crane. 'I really ought to have gone with him.'

'Well for our peace of mind, do you think you ought to go even at this late stage?' said Eliza.

'That would be for the best, I think,' agreed Crane. 'Hopefully nothing untoward has occurred, and the young couple have departed as Davies said.'

So, Crane set off once more for the compound. He rode past the thicket where Regan had tethered his horse and was alarmed at the sight of the animal grazing peacefully.

He galloped at full speed until he reached the group assembled at the canal side.

A relieved Davies greeted him. 'Ah, Mr Crane, thank the Lord you've come. There's a pretty mess on hand here.'

Crane glowered menacingly, 'If there is, I'm sure a lot of it is down to your duplicity in the first place, Davies. Be warned you're skating on very thin ice - now where is Mr. Regan?'

Davies stood his ground defiantly. 'Any actions I took were for sound reasons, good sir. I have reason to believe that the young lady in question has suffered greatly at the hands of her erstwhile master. It seemed my Christian duty to prevent her falling into his clutches again.'

With that, the door of the canteen opened and the two combatants emerged both clad in clean, dry labourer's clothes.

Crane, completely taken aback by the appearance of his gentleman friend gasped, 'What in God's name has happened here. Why is this gentleman so attired?'

No member of the assembled party seemed willing to answer.

Crane persisted, 'Has no-one here a tongue in their head? What skulduggery has taken place?'

It was a much-subdued Regan himself who answered. Although the warm bath had done much to revive him, the near-death experience in the icy murky water had left him in a state of shock and almost overwhelming fatigue.

In a low, almost inaudible murmur, he addressed Crane, 'No-one here is answerable, Godfrey. I'd be obliged if I could prevail upon your goodwill, once more. Please lead me back to your home and I'll explain all. My horse is in yon spinney.'

'Hold hard,' said Davies. 'This man has terrorised a young lass and threatened all here with violence. How do we know he won't try again - he seems of an unsound mind.'

Sam came forward and spoke, 'Let him go in peace Mr Davies. I'm certain he's full of remorse for his deeds and won't be back.'

Turning to Regan he offered his hand, 'I trust you to keep your word, sir, and trouble us no more.'

'I'll do it, Sam, for young Joe's sake,' answered Regan, his voice hoarse with emotion. 'Just tell the lass that my contrition is genuine. She has nothing to fear from me ever again.'

He turned to George Medlock and in a hoarse whisper said, 'Your bravery saved my life and I'll never forget it as long as I live. God bless you, sir.'

Chapter Twenty-Nine

Although only three miles or so back to Danthorp Hall, it was a journey beset with difficulty. Once Crane had retrieved Regan's horse and helped him to mount, he discovered that his companion was hardly able to hold his reins. On several occasions he almost toppled off and Crane had to ride close by his side to prevent that possibility. The warm bath had provided only temporary relief, and the combination of the bitter wind and lack of outer garment soon had Regan shivering uncontrollably with cold again.

The hazardous ride lasted for more than an hour before, at last, the welcome sight of the Hall loomed into view.

Mrs Crane had been waiting anxiously for any sign of her returning husband and, despite her incapacity, was at the door to greet them.

'Oh my, what on earth has happened to Fintan?' she cried.

Regan was helped down by two footmen.

'Let us get him into the warm, and I'll try to explain,' said Crane.

The same servants escorted Regan into the drawing room and settled him on a chaise longue.

Eliza organised blankets to be brought and administered a hot brandy punch, holding the tumbler to Regan's lips. He was shaking so violently he was incapable of holding the glass himself.

Godfrey looked on, his brow furrowed with grave concern.

'This is my understanding of what happened,' he said. 'It seems Fintan's suspicions were well founded. The girl and her husband were still there. There was a violent altercation between Fintan and the young man, and they both finished up in the water. Fintan's attire, including his greatcoat, are presumably still there somewhere.'

'Do you think we should send for Towers?' asked Eliza, anxiously.

'No let's get him to his bed. I think once he thaws out, he'll soon be back to normality.'

Crane continued, 'At least some good has come out of the unfortunate event. He has realised the futility of his quest for once and for all. Let us hope that is the end of the matter. I'm still considering my response to Davies' deceit, however. If he'd told the truth in the first instance, surely this calamity might never have happened.'

'Please don't make a hasty judgment, Godfrey,' replied Eliza. 'I'm sure that Davies was only trying to protect the girl. She was obviously in mortal fear of Mr. Regan, despite his avowed intentions.'

'You may be right, my dear. Let us sleep on it then and see how our guest is in the morning.'

At Preston Brook, the small group who had witnessed the morning's dramatic events were beginning to disperse and go out about what remained of their day's work.

Davies approached the newlyweds, 'I hope never to witness such a sight again, Sam. I pray that we've really seen the last of Mr. Regan.'

'I think he's realised what a hopeless journey he's made and will leave poor Tess in peace,' replied Sam.

'I still think it would be for the best if you took your young bride to meet your family. There's not much work left here anyway, and as I said before, you'll always be welcome back.'

He continued, 'George Medlock and I have a meeting with some important people next week. We're hoping they'll provide finance to start our own small construction company. There's plenty more contracts to bid for, albeit a lot further south.'

'Ay, I think you're right,' answered Sam. 'We've missed today's boat though.'

'Well, here's a proposal for you,' said Davies. 'I told Regan that I'd sold you a horse in lieu of your bonus. It was a lie, of course, but we could make it a reality if you like.'

'Oh, yes!' exclaimed Sam enthusiastically. 'What do you think, Tess?'

Tess, still in a state of bewilderment after the shocking events of the last few days, just nodded her head in agreement.

'Your bonus will be enough to buy my old mare, Bessie. There's a good few years left in her yet, and she's already taken you back twice before, if you recall.'

CHAPTER TWENTY-NINE

'Oh, I do indeed sir!' said Sam. 'She's such a good-natured lady.'

'Now, Mistress Burton, I'm sure if you rode all the way from Wexford to Dublin without a saddle, you could manage another twenty miles or so behind your husband,' said Davies cheerfully. 'Well, that's settled then. Let's hope for a fine day tomorrow for your journey.'

Chapter Thirty

A beautiful sunny morning after a hard frost augured well for the young travellers. Medlock had bequeathed his great-coat to Teresa as a parting gift and Sam had acquired one from the company store, which seemed to stock everything under the sun. The farewell scenes of the previous day, that had been brought to an abrupt end by Regan's dramatic intervention, were repeated, and at last they were on their way.

At the canal junction they turned right and began the twenty or so miles to Barton. They made good progress, passing a steady stream of coal-laden barges going in both directions.

By early afternoon they had reached the mighty aque-duct and began the last stage of their journey, following the same tracks across the fields that had first brought Sam and his brother on their great adventure. It seemed a lifetime ago, so much had changed in Sam's life. Months of hard work had made his body hard and muscular. His hands were calloused, but he had become acclimatised to the discomfort and hardly noticed. Now he was a married man, he wondered what sort of reception his father would give to his young Irish bride. Surely, when he met her, he'd be bowled over by her beauty and sweet innocence and forget the blind prejudice he'd expressed when Sam was last home.

With the daylight of the short winter's day fading rapidly, the Burton smallholding at last came into view and they rode right up to the door of the humble cottage.

Sam thought it a little strange that no-one appeared to have noticed their approach. They dismounted awkwardly, limbs stiff from the long ride. Sam rapped on the door and then opened it and walked into the large room, to be confronted by a pitiful sight. Amy, surrounded by her younger brood of children was sitting at the table, head bowed and crying abjectly.

'Tis me mother, home again,' said Sam, 'but what have I come home to?'

It was young Angela that answered, sobbing, 'Oh, Sam, 'tis father. He's dead.'

A bewildered Sam looked from one to another of his siblings as if seeking confirmation, but none could look at him except baby Peter who ran to him gleefully, at three years old completely unaware of the tragedy that had befallen his family.

Teresa rushed to Sam's side and clung to him.

The door opened again and James, who'd been attending to some tasks in the yard, appeared.

'Ah Sam, welcome home again brother,' he said. 'Tis a hard thing to greet thee.'

'What in God's name has happened and when?' asked Sam urgently.

'He'd been telling us of terrible pains in his head for some weeks, and then early this morning he collapsed in the yard and died at once,' answered James, his voice breaking.

'Where is he now?' asked Sam.

'Still in the yard. I was just getting our John to seek help from Bill Dicey up the lane, when I saw you arrive. Who is this young woman with you?'

'This is Tess. There'll be time for proper introductions later. Let me see father first.'

* * *

The brothers and Teresa went out to where the lifeless body of Seth lay.

Sam shuddered at the sight of his poor father, struck down in his prime. A God-fearing, hard-working countryman whose whole life had been devoted to the care of his wife and family.

A tell-tale trickle of blood from his nose told its tragic tale.

'When he didn't come in for breakfast, I went out to look for him,' said James. 'This is how I found him.'

'At least death must have come quickly,' said Sam, immediately taking control. 'We'll carry him to the outhouse and send for Parson Barlow. No sense in upsetting mother and the bairns more than they already are.'

'Ay, you're right,' agreed James, relieved that his more practical brother had returned right on cue.

Between them the brothers lifted their father's body and laid it as gently as possible on the floor of the lean-to and covered it with some sackcloth. It was the best they could do in the circumstances, until more formal procedures could occur.

'What are we to do, Sam?' said James, his voice still quavering with grief. 'It was so sudden, I thought father would go on for years yet.'

'Well, we'll have to think about what it all means. In the meantime, let's see to Ma and the wee 'uns.'

They returned to the parlour and Sam, crouched by his weeping mother's side, said, 'Ma, 'tis an awful blow fate has dealt us. I'm here now and I'll look after you and the bairns. I've brought someone to meet you.'

Amy raised her head and saw Teresa standing by Sam's side.

'Ma, this is my Tess. We were wed three weeks since and I was bringing her to meet you for Christmas.'

'Oh, Sam. I can't believe it,' sobbed Amy. 'Such a strong hard-working man. How are we to manage without him?'

Looking up at Teresa, she said, 'Welcome, dear girl. I just wish we could have greeted you in a happier circumstance.'

Teresa got on her knees and took Amy's hands in her own.

'I don't know what to say to you. I lost all my family too, so I know something of your grief.'

'Thank you, lass. You must be tired and hungry after your journey. Let me get you some food.'

'Oh no, Mrs Burton. Not now - not just yet.'

'I need something to do,' said Amy. 'Can't sit around moping, it'll not bring him back.'

The usual huge pot of potatoes and turnips was simmering on the hearth, and Amy bade Sam and Teresa to sit at the big table.

She gave them each a dish of the nourishing stew and a hunk of the coarse bread she'd made the previous evening.

'So, you're the Irish girl Sam was so full of last time he was here?'

'I am,' answered Teresa shyly.

'Well, you certainly are a bonny young lass my dear. I can see why my boy wanted you for his wife!'

'Ma,' said Sam. 'I know you and father wanted to see me wed to one of my own as he put it, but my Tess is the sweetest girl in the whole world, and I want no other. She's been through hell in the last twelve months, but we will put all that behind us and will, I know, have a happy life together.'

Amy looked upon them both and said, 'They were your father's words - not mine. I hope you have as good a marriage as my own.' She started to weep again and Teresa rose and embraced her, holding the grieving woman to her bosom as the tears engulfed her.

Thus began a firm and loving relationship between the two women, which was to last until Amy was in her dotage and Teresa was in middle age with four children of her own.

Chapter Thirty-One

At Danthorp, Regan showed no sign of a swift recovery. Despite a huge fire kept permanently in his bedroom and a plenteous supply of blankets, he was still shivering uncontrollably.

Towers attended and administered a dose of laudanum and a herbal elixir, which had little effect other than making him sleep for long periods.

'I fear he may have consumed a copious amount of that foul canal water,' said Towers gravely. 'Together with the exposure to the cold, he may take some time to recover, only time will tell.'

For three days there was no sign of improvement, but on the fourth day he was well enough to take a little food and sit up in bed.

Mrs Crane was in constant attendance, and heartened by the change, she summoned her husband to the bedchamber. 'At last, he seems to be rallying Godfrey.'

'Yes, he's certainly got some colour back,' answered Crane. 'Let us not be over-confident. He's by no means over it yet.'

Over the next few days Regan continued to recuperate, until he was well enough to be up and about.

At breakfast, about a week later, Crane declared, 'Your improving health is a welcome relief, Fintan, but don't make the mistake of trying to leave here too soon. I don't think you're well enough yet.'

'I really can't impose on your kindness for much longer, Godfrey. I have to get back to Warrington and my boy.'

'I have a proposal for you, which has the complete agreement of my wife,' suggested Crane. 'I think we should send for the boy and bring him here. You can spend Christmas with us and think about your homeward journey in the new year, when you have recovered fully.'

'Oh, Godfrey, my dear good man,' replied Regan. 'I have never known such Christian kindness in all my days, but you must allow me to pay you for all the largesse you continue to shower upon me.'

'Nonsense, sir. We have everything we need here and are only too glad to share it. Now let us compose a letter and get it delivered to the Red Lion post haste.'

And so, three days before Christmas, Edward Dunn accompanied by his young charge arrived at Danthorp, and a joyous reunion of father and son took place.

There followed a Christmas period of convivial and satisfying content.

Young Henry was growing in confidence with every day that passed. Under Dunn's excellent stewardship, he was advancing in all aspects, and found himself able to participate in a quite serious and intelligent manner with the conversations of his elders.

He learned of his father's success in finding the fugitives, and the tragic and disastrous outcome, although he was spared the gruesome details of Regan's final denouement.

He was already becoming an astute observer of others' emotional moods, and he noticed a much-changed demeanour in his father. He seemed to Henry, to have acquired an air of dejection - a defeated man given to long spells of silent contemplation.

Henry had been told of poor Joe's sad death, but his father's unsuccessful pursuit of Mary was scarcely referred to, and Henry, shrewdly, kept his thoughts to himself on the whole business.

* * *

On the last day of the year a heavy snowfall followed by a period of bitter cold days and hard frosty nights drove all thought of any early departure from their minds.

The Regans and Dunn had no choice but to enjoy the hospitality of their hosts, until well into February.

During that time there was a slow, steady improvement in Regan's health, both physically and mentally.

Godfrey Crane had made another friend in the studious Edward Dunn. They were often observed having long earnest discussions about the efficacy of the canal network that was being established.

'The whole creation will bring nothing but great prosperity to the whole nation,' declared Crane.

'Yes,' agreed Dunn. 'I can see the advantages, but what of the pitfalls? I've heard and read of much opposition in certain quarters.'

'All tosh and tomfoolery,' scoffed Crane. 'Small-minded selfish landowners who cannot bear to have their estates invaded for the common good.'

Such conversation was the mainstay of many an evening spent in the cosy warmth of Crane's study where the three men were usually ensconced after dinner. At first, Regan was content to listen to the discourses of his host and secretary, but as his health improved, he began to put forward some of his own thoughts. Meanwhile, Eliza entertained young Henry in the drawing room, with rudimentary piano lessons or teaching him the rules of such card games as whist and Quadrille.

Regan gradually came to the conclusion that his futile mission may not have been in vain after all. He would never have met the Cranes or the estimable Edward Dunn and would have remained in total ignorance of these grand canal plans. He was also disturbed by the effect that Crane's beautiful young wife was having on him. He tried in vain to ignore these quite treacherous thoughts. He was no nearer solving the mystery of what seemed to him a gross mismatch. They were obviously very fond of one another. Maybe it was a common occurrence in this alien country for a man to take a much younger wife. He'd lost his obsession with Mary in the icy depths of the canal. His previous callous attitude to the female sex, he'd also left behind. He knew that any attempt at revealing his ardour towards the lady in question would only lead to embarrassment and estrangement, so with difficulty kept these feelings to himself.

He grew increasingly restless as the days began to lengthen, and as February drew to a close, plans were made to return to Warrington and find a passage back to Dublin.

On the morning of their departure, Regan addressed his hosts from the saddle of his horse

'I thank the Lord for directing me to your door Eliza and Godfrey. I'll never forget your hospitality to a complete stranger. True Christian people, who have given me food for thought as to how I must change my ways, still further. I know you would never accept money from me, and I wouldn't insult your dignity by insisting upon it.'

He drew a purse of money from his saddlebag and handed it to Eliza saying, 'Please share this among the poor of your parish. Let us stay in touch through regular correspondence, my dear friends.'

With one last look at the woman who would never be his, he wheeled his horse round and set off for Warrington.

Soon afterwards as they breasted a hill, Regan bade his companions to stop for a moment's reflection. Looking down at the distant Danthorp Hall, he said, 'Come Henry and Edward. Let us return to Wexford and who knows, maybe we can build a mighty canal of our own!'

Chapter Thirty-Two

Christmas at the humble Burton farmstead was in total contrast to the one enjoyed at Danthorp.

Seth's funeral took place at St. Margarets on Christmas Eve and set the mood for a miserable festive season.

Amy had offered her bed to the newlyweds, but to Sam and Teresa that notion was unthinkable, and so they slept on the floor of the main room, under their greatcoats.

There was at least meat in abundance. The pig purchased by Seth in the summer had duly fattened and been slaughtered by Jack King, the pigman. The hams and other cuts were smoked and hung in his store.

On New Year's Day, despite the harsh weather, James and Sam were summoned to the church, where in the vestry, Robert Mitchell - one of the Duke's many stewards - presented James with a new tenancy agreement.

James, as first born, was to be allowed to continue in his father's stead.

Addressing Sam, Mitchell said, 'I understand that you have been employed on the great canal project. Is this true?'

'It is true,' answered Sam. 'I returned home for the holiday on the very day of my father's untimely death. My intention was to return to Preston Brook, but sadly that plan has gone awry.'

'Yes, fate has dealt your family a cruel blow,' said Mitchell. 'However, as the saying goes, when one door closes another one opens. I have proposal for you, Mr Burton.'

'What would that be?' asked Sam cautiously.

Mitchell continued, 'The Duke himself has instructed me to deal favourably with all canal employees. There is a holding, only two miles or so from your own, where an old widow woman, Rose Adnitt, is struggling to survive alone. I could draw up a new tenancy for yourself, which would entail you taking over from her but allowing her to stay on and share the dwelling.'

'Rose Adnitt is my aunt through marriage,' said Sam. 'I know well enough how she is in a woeful state. It would be an honour to help her.'

Sam had already come to ruefully accept the fact that his life as a canal builder had come to an end. He couldn't possibly leave his brother to cope alone, especially as James, too, was betrothed and would need a home for his new wife.

* * *

By Easter, a full year after his great canal adventure had begun, Sam Burton reflected upon the great changes in his life in just one year.

He was a happily married man, with a pregnant young wife - a tenant farmer in his own right. The skills he'd learned at the hands of Medlock and other craftsmen had enabled him to start building another dwelling on his farm, using materials purchased with some of their combined fortune. Small though it was, it had proved adequate to furnish their immediate needs with some left over to help his grieving mother and young siblings

He worked in close harmony with his brother James and between them the two farms were already at an advanced stage of planting.

All in all, he was content with his lot in life, but at times couldn't help reflecting on what might have been if he'd stayed the course with Medlock and Davies.

He kissed his darling Tess, patted her swelling stomach and prepared for another day on his new farm.

In the evening by candlelight, he composed a letter with paper and pen acquired from Parson Barlow.

Epilogue

Preston Brook tunnel was finally finished, and navigation became possible along almost the entire length of the Trent and Mersey canal in 1777.

The magnificent feat of engineering, a ninety-three-mile navigation between Preston Brook and Derwent Mouth near Derby, contained five tunnels and 70 locks. It provided a link between the ports of Liverpool on the west coast and Hull on the east coast. By the 1820's, other canals such as the Shropshire Union, the Coventry and the Oxford made it possible to ship goods between all parts of England, including London, Birmingham and Bristol, entirely by water. Thus was James Brindley's grand ambition achieved, although he didn't live to see it. He died in 1772.

The compound at Preston Brook was no longer needed, although some of the buildings were converted into warehousing and a toll office.

The unsung heroes, the workforce, were paid off and dispersed in various directions, to find work where they could.

Some of the locals went back to their farm labouring, but for the vast majority, itinerants from far afield, it meant a period of uncertainty. Their hard-earned wages rapidly dispensed with, some followed the canal towpath to the burgeoning settlements of Manchester and Salford to seek work in the new factories and cotton mills. For some, however, the future was more assured.

Davies and Medlock had indeed started their own small construction company, with a working capital of £500 provided by a consortium of forward-thinking businessmen. A substantial part of that capital had been put up by Godfrey Crane. He'd concluded that Davies' part in Regan's downfall was perfectly understandable. In fact, it was he that had put together the consortium. He was the chief contributor with smaller investments from Towers the surgeon, and Eliza's brother, Frederick Wallace.

There was still work for some at the Preston Brook complex for an unspecified time. Despite the bitter winter weather, the fledgling company secured a contract to dismantle some of the buildings and arrange for the onward shipment of bricks, timber and other essentials.

Medlock had persuaded his trusty workforce to stay with him, promising work for the foreseeable future. The Donegal men and their wives were more than ready to oblige, seeing no prospect of returning to their native land.

Davies had not been idle and by the springtime had secured a contract to dig a section of the new Caldon canal. With the modest profit from their first venture, they purchased picks, shovels and wheelbarrows from the Trent and Mersey Company, and sent them by boat to Etruria, where the junction was to be made.

As April drew to a close, and final arrangements for the new venture were nearing completion, a letter arrived addressed to George Medlock.

He read it through carefully and then shared its content with Davies and the workmen.

Dear Mr. Medlock.

I expect you are wondering why we didn't return, but fate has intervened and changed the course of our lives. On the very day of our leaving you all, we returned to find that my father had dropped down dead. The surgeon said it was a haemorrhage of the brain. I had no option open to me than to stay here and care for my mother and young bairns.

Since then, I have obtained the tenancy of my own small farm, and so I have to say that we will not be joining you after all. Tess is with child and God willing will present me with a son or daughter in October. We'll never forget the time we spent helping to build that mighty waterway, and the lessons I learned from you, George.

I have been able to put my experiences to use and have built a small dwelling on my farm for my new family. We've had our share of misfortune but hope to put it all behind us. We wish you all the best of luck for whatever the future may hold for you.

May God bless you.

Respectfully yours,

Sam and Teresa

Afterthoughts

So, this tale comes to an end. It is mostly a figment of my imagination, interspersed with some real names from history, i.e., the Duke of Bridgewater, James Brindley and Josiah Wedgwood.

The inspiration came whilst I was completing a charity walk, I undertook in the summer of 2021.

I wanted to raise money for my local hospice, St. Mary's in Ulverston, where my poor brave wife, Sheila, finally lost her seventeen-year battle with Parkinsons Disease.

I decided to combine my love of walking with my lifelong interest in our wonderful canal system. I walked the whole length of the Oxford canal to Hawkesbury Junction and then carried on along the Coventry for five miles to its terminus in the canal basin in the city centre.

As I walked every day, I marvelled at the ingenuity of James Brindley, William Jessop and Thomas Telford to name but a few. Their foresight and acumen laid the foundations of a network that has stood the test of time for 250 years. The massive undertaking, mostly completed in the period from the 1770's to the 1820's, was constructed by men using nothing more than picks and shovels. On one of the stages of my walk, I was accompanied by my granddaughter Stacey, my stepson Jonathan, and his partner Sarina. They had never seen a canal lock in their lives, and I took great pleasure in informing them that they were watching eighteenth century technology at work and still going strong!

The network was a major component in the Industrial Revolution, enabling the transport of vast quantities of goods and materials from one end of the country to the other. Despite the decline brought about by first the railways and then the internal combustion engine, they are thriving. Thanks largely to the dedication of bands of canal enthusiasts, huge parts of the network have been restored. Sadly, they are no longer used for the purpose for which they were built but have developed into the multi-billion leisure cruising industry of today.

I used various reference books for research, the most notable of which were; *Waterways in the Making* by Edward Paget Tomlinson - an invaluable little book complete with hand sketches of various construction methods. Anthony Burton's work, *The Canal Builders* was another great source of inspiration.

I would like to thank Emma Huck for proof reading and editing my work.

Ingram Content Group UK Ltd.
Milton Keynes UK
UKHW010830190423
420414UK00006B/656